Hannah's Journey

By Carmen Peone

Carmen Peone

ISBN-13:

ISBN-10:

Cover design and formatting by Rossano Designs

Published by Painted Hill Press

Praise for *Hannah's Journey*

I found *Hannah's Journey* an absorbing, well-written book, a story intriguing to a wide audience. The author speaks with authority about Indian history, and the Sinyekst people. Peone is knowledgeable about the northeast Washington area, the Columbia River and the diverse area surrounding it.

– *Mary Trimble, Author*

The story is more powerful because while these young people attend to the serious business of survival, they retain a playfulness and humor that is contagious and entertaining.

– *Anne Schroeder, Award Winning author and speaker*

Books by Carmen Peone

Gardner Sibling Trilogy

Delbert's Weir

Heart Trilogy

Change of Heart

Heart of Courage

Heart of Passion

Dedication

To girls with big dreams.

Trust in the LORD with all your heart and

lean not on your own understanding.

Proverbs 3:5

Chapter 1

Northeast Washington Territory, 1870

He marched toward me as though off to battle. Long braids thumped his bare chest with each step. His eyes glistened in the afternoon sun, tugging my attention to his bold posture and sharp-edged face. My gaze dropped to his pursed lips and clenched jaw and I groaned, eyes searching for somewhere to hide because in reality, he was my enemy. At every opportunity he made his opinions loud and lucid—girls like me should not race against Indian boys. I rubbed the light skin on the back of my hand. He strutted up to me, keeping his gaze on mine, mouth opened.

My gaze darted from side to side and as I realized my show of fear, I planted my feet, lifted my chin, and stared back at him, knees quivering.

"Why are you still here?" Wind Chaser said.

He glared at me with coal-colored, wide-set eyes. For a minute I thought he might raise a hand and strike me. I took a couple steps back, hoping I was out of reach. He stole those steps back, coming closer than before. I squinted my eyes and curled my upper lip, taking a moment to gain a speck of control before answering.

"Because I'm racing today." I leaned close and got a whiff of his sweet-venison breath. "Like you." I stood tall, turned, and walked off.

"You are not as strong a rider as your *Sinyekst* aunt!" Wind Chaser cackled.

I whisked past him, bumping his shoulder. I pulled up my brother's tattered britches hidden under my skirt as I marched to my horse. My belt had broken just before departing for the race, leaving me no time to hunt for a replacement. Now I wished I'd taken the time. I hated the confinement of suspenders and refused to wear them, certain my Indian aunt had an old piece of buckskin laying around that would suffice.

No one was going to talk me out of racing. *No one!* I may be a brown-haired girl in britches, but at sixteen years of age I was woman enough to handle this affair. I glanced over at my horse. With ears pricked forward, she was alert and ready. Hands on thin hips, I breathed in deep, then exhaled the insults.

"What did he say to you this time?" Falling Rain coughed and handed me my horse's reins. After a long bout with a sore throat and fever, her normally dark skin paled her round face. Shadows masked her tired-looking eyes. She had remained with her father while the rest of the women went into the mountains to pick huckleberries. This gave her time with the grumpy healer to learn more about native medicines.

I shook my head. "Nothin' new."

"Then why do you look like he pulled your pigtails and threw dirt in your face?"

I shrugged. "He said I will never be as strong a rider as my aunt."

Falling Rain shuddered. "He is lower than a snake's

belly and you know nothing is lower than a snake's belly."

I cringed. "And nothing smarter either."

Falling Rain hugged me and boosted me up on my leggy mare, Moonie.

I nodded at her. "Reckon it's time to give these boys a respectable lickin' they'll never forget."

"Be careful." She stepped back.

I spun my horse around and found my way to the other racers. I scanned the area to examine my competition. Not much for men. Seven scrawny, dark-skinned boys slouched on top of their horses. They all rode bareback and bare-chested with buckskin leggings and moccasins. The only one riding in a saddle, I set my boots deep in the stirrups.

The Indian boys glared at me. One spit on the ground next to Moonie's front foot. Another raised an arm, war-whooping and screaming Sinyekst at me. His words sounded harsh, like when whites used curse words when riled. I recognized "stupid dog," "go home," and "woman's work," My skin crawled as I fought the urge to retaliate. I bit my tongue in order to obey Pa's words of wisdom—never quarrel with a fool! Wind Chaser sat on his horse and glared at me. My fear of him shifted to hate.

White knuckled, I reined my horse into the spot I thought we might begin.

The other racers pointed and laughed. Then they moved into position a ways north where a wide meadow stood between the mountains and the Columbia River.

I lifted my chin and followed them, pinning my sights on the trail that disappeared through the woods. I rubbed Moonie's neck. "We can beat these no-accounts."

Falling Rain tucked herself between a couple of younger cousins who wore doeskin dresses that fell below their knees; long, black braids hung over thin shoulders, their feet black with dirt. She smiled, giving me a look of encouragement. I nodded, then stared at the tree line in front of me.

A loud *thwack* from a hand drum bayed on a slight breeze. I kicked Moonie. She lunged forward, instantly ahead of the others. Her hooves chewed up the prairie grass, kicking dirt in her wake. We made our way to the forest edge, wound through trees and hog-sized rocks, and climbed up a steep hill. I passed one boy as we crested the hill. He grabbed at the collar of my dress, but I managed to wiggle out of his grip.

At the base of the hill, we jumped over a creek. While one horse balked, I shot past him like an arrow out of a tightly strung bow. We galloped through trees and around a bend, turning back in the direction where we began. Moonie crept up on Wind Chaser's horse, her breaths coming hard and fast. "You can do it." I kicked hard. Her legs stretched forward with each step.

Wind Chaser glanced back, a look of surprise swept across his face.

By the time we galloped past the spear marking the finish line, it was not enough. I circled Moonie down to a walk as the others straggled in. *I almost had him!* My body shook as adrenaline surged through me. Racers bumped their horses into mine, unquestionably on purpose. From the beginning, threats and insults made it clear I'd not been welcome.

Wind Chaser rode up beside me. "Stay home. You will never beat me."

"Stay home!" The others chanted in their own

language. They also made references to cooking and sewing. I figured the Good Lord would not have put this desire in me if it wasn't what he'd wanted. I was certain of that. Aunt Spupaleena had cleared the way for me years ago, and I figured it was up to me to keep that path open for those yet to come.

One boy grabbed my wrists, holding tight. "If you try and race again, we'll take it out on your little sister!" He laughed and rode off.

"Touch her and I'll kill you!" I swatted at him with my rein and lifted a hand for a second go at him, but was blocked by another Indian boy whose scarred face resembled a shadow of death. His dark-brown eyes pricked at me like a serpent's twisted lies. My gut told me to spin Moonie around and kick. Yet I stared at the boy, unable to move.

"You do not belong here," another Indian boy said.

I studied him. "Who are you?" He looked familiar. I leaned closer. "What's your name?" *Where do I know him from?*

"I am a friend of Wind Chaser—"

"Friend?" I grunted. "Didn't know the sidewinder had friends."

He sneered at me. "My name is Silent Thunder—"

"Is there such a thing?" I said.

"Stay home! Or you will be hurt." He kicked his horse, ramming him into Moonie.

I slapped him with my reins until he backed away. "Stay away from me!"

Wind Chaser crowded me and in a low, snarl said, "Listen to us. Or you will not come out of the woods alive."

I raised my hand to slap him across the face, but Wind Chaser grabbed it, twisting my wrist.

"Let go, you—"

"Hannah Gardner!" Mama's footsteps kept the same pace as Uncle Pekam's hand drum during ceremonies. "What are you doing?"

"Think about what I have said." Wind Chaser shoved my wrist, turned, and trotted away.

I dismounted and wiped the sweat off my brow with the sleeve of my shirtwaist.

"What are you wearing? Britches under your new calico skirt? This is absurd! No lady dresses nor acts in this manner. No daughter of mine, that is. Who is that boy and didn't your pa and I tell you no more racing?" Mama set her hands on her hips. Her slight frame was no comparison for the growl in her voice.

My gaze dropped to the ground. "Yes, ma'am, you did tell me no more racing." I pushed dirt around with the toe of my boot. "But I know I can ride as well as Aunt Spupaleena—"

"Hannah! Listen to me." Mama placed a hand on my shoulder. "You know we are not like the Sinyekst. They come from the Arrow Lakes way up north in Canada. They are strong and—"

"And I'm just as—"

"That's not what I mean." Mama sighed. "We love them like family even though we are not blood. But we have different customs and practices. They have their ways and we have ours. No better, simply different. And yes, you are an accomplished rider. Darling, there is no future for a young lady like you to race horses. Your future is with a husband and raising children. That's the way things are. Please—"

"No! Those are your plans, not mine. You know I'd rather be in a saddle than bent over an iron stove, stirring a pot of beans." I rubbed my wrist. "Yes, someday I want to have a husband and children, but for now, I wanna race. I know how to garden, quilt, sew, tend to the sick. You've taught me those skills. Let me do this before I choose to settle down."

Mama shook her head and with fear in her voice said, "No!" She took hold of my wrist. "Now come along. We're going out with Smilkameen to gather herbs. Learn more about their medicinal purposes." She tried to tug me by her side.

"Ouch!" I pulled free and ran back to Moonie for a second race. "Watch me, Mama. I'll prove to you how good I am," I shouted over my shoulder.

"Hannah, if you get on that horse and ride, I will find a girl's boarding school for you back east. Remember, that's where my roots are. There is always Aunt Erma's in Montana. That would be more suitable."

Her words stopped me from mounting. I faced her, upper lip curled. "Is it Elizabeth Gardner's way or no way? My dreams have no importance?" The stench of soaking deer brains matched how I felt about my mama's will at that moment. She took a step toward me. I took a step back.

"I did not raise you to speak to me that way." Her chin trembled. She sighed. "Yes, your dreams have meaning. We all have freedom to plan and dream. But with that freedom we have responsibilities. We cannot run wild like a tumbleweed in whichever direction the breeze blows us. When I crossed this land as a mail-order bride to meet your father, I was filled with fear. I knew with the death of my folks, I needed a change so I wouldn't go mad. I had plans and dreams of my own. But I chose to swallow my pride and see the path ahead as an adventure into untamed territory. I chose to roll up my sleeves, leave my fashionable dresses with cousins, and make a life for myself. Out here with your father, we've made a respectable life. A happy one. We have a better life than I could have ever imagined had I remained in Virginia. A home. Love."

I could tell she was fighting tears. At the same time I had a notion to stand my ground. A storm brewed in me I'd never felt before. My hands sweat, and my face felt blazing hot. "But that's your life, Mama. Not mine." My voice squeaked.

Mama dropped her gaze and sighed. "You are difficult and stubborn. I'll remind you of your options. Come with me now, or off to boarding school you go."

Falling Rain cleared her throat. "Hannah, they are waiting for you."

I nodded.

Mama squared her shoulders. "Hannah, put your horse away. I *will* see you and Falling Rain back at the village." Mama lifted her green skirt that matched the shade of her eyes and headed for Spupaleena's tule lodge.

I turned to Falling Rain. "I'm ready."

"What is a girls' school?"

"A prison, and I'm dead certain I'll never set foot in one."

Chapter 2

Coyotes howled into early morning. I tossed and turned, sifting through reasons why my folks settled on sending me away. Especially after winning the second race by beating Wind Chaser. They acted like I'd murdered someone. All I did was race a horse.

It'd been two days since I raced. Mama kept to herself and her Bible. Pa spent most of his time praying and complaining to the Lord about having an unruly daughter. The look on his face when Mama came storming home about broke my heart. But still…

"I don't even know Aunt Erma in Montana," I said to Lillian's doll. I glanced at the doll Mama had given her last Christmas. She wore a pink and white gingham dress, which she'd made to match one of Lillian's, and yellow yarn hair. Pink buttons formed eyes and red yarn stitched a mouth.

I shook my head at the thought of living with someone I'd not yet been acquainted with. I do not recall Mama mentioning her prior with her disappointment in me. I am almost certain she is an imaginary threat. Something my folks are using to keep me corralled. But I am like a wild horse. I cannot be penned up. Not for long anyhow. Mama mentioned her age.

In her sixties? "Aunt Erma is too old to care for me. What will we do? Sit around and quilt?" I shook the doll's head. "How will I get there? Stage coach?" I nodded the doll's head. "Nah. Delbert would have to take me. But I reckon he can't. There's too much work to be done around here. Plus he's only thirteen." I pressed my lips against the doll's imaginary ear. "On the other hand, he's old enough to take over all the chores." I grunted. "Aunt Erma's too old to keep up." My fingers make the doll's head move up and down. "You see things my way, don't ya."

I groaned. "The other choice is to stay with Pa's friend and his family up north in Pinkney City." I vaguely remembered meeting the Grahams. Besides, they talked funny. Mama said they're Irish, straight off the boat from Ireland. But I still won't go there. Even if it's the closest place to stay. "How could they send me away? I'm kin. Their flesh and blood." I tossed the doll on Lillian's bed. "Reckon it's time." I shuffled out to the kitchen table like a wounded bird and plopped down on a chair beside my father.

The way Pa fiddled with his rope and stared at me intermittently made me sink deeper in the chair. Mama scrubbed the table from the morning meal. We seemed to be waiting for her. We, as in me, her, and Pa. Delbert went on ahead to check cattle down in the valley. Lillian was sent to feed the pigs and gather eggs even though Mama got them all this morning. Reckon Mama knew she'd lose herself to the animals in the barn. Dry lightning flittered about in our little cabin, the kind right before the thunder booms. I figured an explosion was about to happen.

Mama took her time putting plates and cups away in

their tidy rows on tidy shelves. Every item had its place in the cabin. Jars of dried herbs lined the ledge beside the iron stove. Flowered curtains hung straight. Wild flowers perched in a vase in the center of the table, not one inch off. Quilts lay flat and square on beds. She fiddled and hummed. I reckoned she was planning her attack with precision. As a miner places dynamite in the exact location.

Once Mama finished, she untied her apron, hung it on the hook, and sat down with us at the table. Pa placed his rope on the floor then glanced at her before pinning his sights on me. I understood then how a deer might feel once he sees the rifle pointed at his head. I dropped my gaze to a knot on the table.

"Hannah, I'm disappointed in the way you treated your mother at the village."

I lifted my eyes up enough to peek through my lashes. "Yes, sir."

"After much discussion, we think perhaps you need to go and stay with family in Montana. It would be for a year. Maybe more."

I swayed, felt like I'd topple off my chair. My arm caught the ledge of the table. I closed my eyes. Swayed some more. I heard a slap on the table and opened my eyes to Pa's rope before me. An imagined noose made for hefty threats.

"We've told you many times racing is dangerous and not ladylike. Your skirts flying up like they do, showing man's britches. It's not right." Pa shook his head. "It was one thing when you were five and six. Things are different now."

I leaned forward, hands on the table. "Why would you take Spupaleena in as a young girl, broken and bruised, a run-away, heal her, treat her like she's your own daughter, give her a horse and send her off to fulfill her desires? Why her and not me?"

Pa combed his hair with his fingers. "That was different—"

I leaned back. "How?" I was tired of hearing those declarations.

"Racing was her salvation. She needed something after losing her mother and brother. She needed something to hang on to. To live for. Two deaths in a short time, that's too much for anyone." Pa raised his brows. "Not to mention later going home to find her sister and grandmother had passed on." He fingered his rope. "Besides, she was never ours. We had to let her go."

I wrung my hands in my lap.

Mama cleared her throat. "Hannah, things are different with you. Times and cultures, they have unique situations and expectations. This is the only way to get you to stop behaving like a boy. Racing's got too tight a hold on you." She fingered her blue and green flower embroidered tea towel. "You don't seem to be listening to us." Her voice broke.

I shook my head. "I don't want to stop racing. You always talk to Aunt Spupaleena about being a strong woman and fighting for her dreams—"

Pa pounded his fist on the table, making both Mama and me jump. "That's enough!" He took a deep breath. "You will not speak to your mother like that, and you will obey us or it's off to Montana with Aunt Erma. I've already spoken with Jack Dalley. He's willing to escort you there."

I knew Jack, our neighbor and Pa's best friend, would have no trouble helping to get rid of me. Maybe this was their way to work with Spupaleena more and me less. If they could get rid of me, they'd have their girl. Their strong Indian girl. They'd been with her from the beginning. Heck, Jack had given Spupaleena the horse that started her herd. A big Paint. He made her famous in these parts.

Mama lifted her chin, water glimmering in her eyes. "We'll give you time to weigh your options. We'll talk more after supper tonight."

I raced out of the cabin and to the corral. I saddled Moonie and kicked hard. Tears streamed down my cheeks as the wind slapped my face. I didn't run her very far. Only enough for the pressure to loosen its grip from around my throat. We walked for several miles before spotting our cows beside a creek. I scanned the area for Delbert, but there was no sign of him. Knowing my brother, he was scoutin' the hills for small game, not paying attention to strays while the herd plodded down the dusty trail.

I dismounted, led Moonie to the creek, and splashed cool water on my face and neck. My mare clambered in and drank. "Gotta make a plan, Moonshine. I will not let them take you from me and everything I know. I have to prove I can race and ride as good as the rest of 'em—and win. That'll change their minds." I plopped down on the grass. "Spupaleena had to prove herself and so can I." I fingered my auburn-colored locks. "Ladies can ride just as well as the boys."

I lay back in the grass, arms covering my forehead. July storms tended to roll in quickly—vulgar and unforgiving—hidden behind the mountains. Several clouds threatened their wrath. I closed my eyes, a fist around Moonie's reins. "Who is Aunt Erma? Would it be me and her? How long would it take to get there?" I cringed, imagining an old, cranky lady with a cane and tattered apron. "Can I race in Montana?" I groaned. "Probably not." I sat up and tossed a stone into the creek.

I let Moonie graze a spell before getting up and combing her mane with my fingers. Her real name was Moonshine. I, of course, had not named her. Mama would have tanned my hide if I came home calling her something that heathen. Pa said the name came with the horse. He had fidgeted like a toddler with a wet diaper when she asked about the mare's name. He explained it was not after bootleg, but the shine of a full moon reflecting off the Columbia River. I called her Moonie. Her dappled Palomino color was soft and warm and she was as quiet as a kitten. And just as confident.

Once as a young girl, I'd overheard Pa mention rich soil and pasture land in Montana territory to Jack. He said it was prime cattle country with open prairies and big skies. Jack disputed that the Washington territory was new and exciting. Untamed. I agreed with Jack.

In these parts whites were barely scattered in between Indian tribes and everyone lived peacefully. Most non-Indians planted their roots in forts or small towns like Pinkney City. I didn't know if there were Indians in Montana. I suspected so and figured they were more'n likely agreeable, similar to the ones around here. I prayed they weren't the warrin' kind. Trappers at the Kettle Falls talked about warrin' Indians that mutilated others and themselves. I was not about to live near such horror.

This was the territory I planned on growing my roots deep. Where pine trees and wildflowers filled the air. I plucked a few needles from the ground, rubbed my palms over them, and sniffed. "Mmmm." Was Montana this beautiful? Or was it filled with sand and sagebrush? Today the air smelled of a storm comin'. A gust of wind blew stray hair in my face. Fields of wildflowers waved purple, pink, yellow, and white. I stood, searching for Delbert. If lightning was anywhere close, we'd have to hurry back.

Hoof beats pounded in the distance. I gathered my skirts and mounted, wishing I had Delbert's britches on. A cow and calf pair turned the corner, coming into view with my brother hot on their tails.

I grabbed hold of Moonie's reins and twirled her around, heading off the big-eyed pair. They headed toward the rest of the herd. Cows circled around, spraying dirt in all directions. Calves sprinted forward a few steps and found their mothers again. They bawled, seeming to search for an escape route, but Delbert rounded them up and drove them to the creek.

"Thanks for the help," Delbert said once the cows were settled and back to grazing. "What are ya doing out here?"

I looked away. "Thinkin'."

"About what?"

"Decisions I have to make."

"So I heard." Delbert gave me a snarky grin. "Figure it out yet?"

I lifted my chin. "I surely have."

"How's that?" Delbert coiled his rope and tied it on the side of the saddle below the horn.

"I understand why they don't want me to race, but I'm old enough to decide for myself. And it's no concern of yours!"

Delbert stared at me, opened mouthed. He waved his face with his Stetson and shook his head. "And I thought

I was the stubborn one."

"Stubborn? How is wanting to chase after my dreams stubborn?" A drop of water hit my face. Clouds the color of a deep bruise hovered.

"Part of being a woman is holding on to responsibility. Sounds like you have a long ways to go, sister." Delbert plopped his cowboy hat back on his head. "You can start now by helping me move these cattle up to Drifter's Meadow before the storm hits.

"You sound like Pa." I spit dirt on the ground, wiping the rest on my shirtsleeve.

Delbert and his dirt-covered face circled around the herd and pushed them toward me. Lightning cracked to the east, far enough away the cows only jumped, then continued to graze. I held my breath, praying they wouldn't stampede and run me over. We headed out—me in the lead and Delbert riding drag. From there we pushed fifty-two head south—twenty-five cow and calf pairs and two ornery bulls of stink and slobber.

The sun settled high to the west when we stopped for a break. My belly growled. "Got anything to eat?"

Delbert fished hardtack out of his saddlebag and handed me a piece. "I should let you starve the way you've back talked Ma."

I ripped off a hunk and chewed. "You ain't so perfect. Don't got much brains either. As I recall, you and Ross forgot most of your food and fishin' hooks on your little adventure last month."

Delbert blushed. "I s'pose we did." He chewed a piece, handing over his canteen. "But I never spoke to Ma like a spoiled brat." He pointed south. "We'll drive the herd over those two hills and into the next valley. There's plenty of grass and a nice waterhole."

An eagle soared overhead, then dove into the Columbia River and scooped up a fish in its talons. He floated freely above the water. I wanted to be that limitless. Free to make my own decisions. As the eagle circled overhead, I knew what was next.

I'd have to soar low.

Chapter 3

The outline of the barn came into view as I rounded the corner of our log cabin. It was still dark and the rooster hadn't yet called for us to wake up. Moonie snorted, leading the rest of the horses in their ravenous chant. I stopped mid-stride, glancing around to make certain I was still the only one out here. Then I continued to the corral. Moonie ate the handful of grass I offered her. I tossed a bit of hay to silence the rest of the animals. I saddled my mare and led her out of the corral, walking as fast as I could without making a racket. I pulled my Stetson low, like a robber, and cinched my horsehair string snug under my chin.

A tap on a window caught my attention. I froze. Lillian waved at me, sleep creasing her face. Reddish-brown curls, the color of tamarack bark, framed her petite features. She wiped strays from her eyes. I tapped my lips with my finger and tiptoed forward. *Lord, for once, let her keep her mouth closed.*

When hidden in the woods, I stepped into the saddle and kicked Moonie into a trot. By the time the sun crowned the mountains, I came to the section of the Columbia River that was safest to cross. After Moonie took a nice long drink, she swam us across. We traveled a ways north to the Sinyekst village. Tule-pit lodges lined the river bank, smoke swirling from the top. Kids played with sticks and dolls, while women cooked and men visited. We waved at one another as I rode through, and then veered west. The smell of morning cooking fires wafted through the air. Up a hill and settled in a valley perched Spupaleena's tule lodge.

The crunch of horse hooves on twigs sounded in the distance. I squinted, unable to see anyone at first, then Spupaleena came into view. Legs relaxed yet steady, she rode bareback with a single rope around the jaw of her horse. She trotted one of her race horses in and out of the trees. They rode in smooth unison, appearing to float like clouds. The horse's golden brown coat glistened in the sun as they stepped out of the trees and crossed the meadow. The fringe on her doeskin dress danced to the beat of each hoof.

Behind her Pekam exercised a Paint horse. I recognized the horse, Dancing Chicken, because the marking on the animal's neck resembled a rooster with one leg lifted in the air. Pekam's long braids bounced off his bare back. He rode like his sister—no saddle and one thin rope around the jaw controlling the stallion. My uncle's knees clung to the horse as they galloped circles in knee-high grass.

I rode closer, staying clear of their path, wishing I could ride as well as my Indian relatives. Moonie pricked her ears forward as my aunt came close, then swiveled them toward my uncle as she rode off. Back and forth they went. I waved. Spupaleena nodded. I rode Moonie close to my aunt's lodge and tied her to a tree. Even with all the commotion, she cocked a hind leg and dropped her head. I picked a couple handfuls of grass and offered her a taste. She sniffed before eating them. "You are a swell girl, Moonie."

My adopted aunt and uncle cooled off their horses as temperatures rose. Pekam put one horse away and chose another.

Spupaleena waved me over. "Untie Moonie." She took a long drink out of a dried deer bladder.

We walked the horses to a nearby creek and led them into rushing water. It felt good on my bare feet. I splashed water on my neck, set my hat on the bank, and wet my braided hair. "Your mare is looking good."

Spupaleena dipped her hands in the water and let it run over her horse's back. She did this several times before speaking. "Yes, she feels strong. I will race her in five suns." She rubbed more water over the horse's muscles, speaking softly in her Sinyekst tongue. It sounded more like a prayer.

When she'd finished I asked, "I was hoping I could ride and train with you for a spell."

Again she paused, near as I could figure asking the Lord for wisdom before answering, as she normally did. Especially when she felt something was amiss. Since I generally didn't show up alone, I'm confident she saw this as wayward.

"Does your *toom* and *mistum* know where you are?"

At first I nodded. Then shook my head. "I suspect by the conversations we've had the past couple days, they realize I've come here."

Spupaleena lifted a brow. "You know you cannot run off when you get angry. When you do not get what you want."

"But they're gonna send me off to Aunt Erma's in

Montana. I don't even know her, but I do know my place is on the back of a horse, like you." I fought back tears. "I won't leave."

Spupaleena leaned against her horse and closed her eyes. Her lips moved. I waited until she was ready to speak, planning some form of retaliation of my own in case she'd try and convince me to return home.

She opened her eyes and turned to me. "You may stay."

"I can?" Was this a trick? I figured she'd put up more of a fight than that. Or was her plan to make things so tough on me I'd go crawling back to my folks like a scolded dog with its tail between its legs.

"*Kewa.* I will help you. Only this one time." She chuckled. "I was your age once. Your folks helped me. I know you feel the same way as I do about racing, and I know you will not stop until you have answers. So I will help you. *Naux.*" She held up one finger.

I hugged her. "Thank you. I knew you'd understand. It's in our blood. You and me. Racing, it's who we are."

She shook her head. "*Loot, Kook Yuma Mahooya.* Not who we are. What we do." She brushed hair out of my face. "When I think you are ready, we will have your naming ceremony."

"You've never called me that before. What does it mean?"

"It means little raccoon. You always test the water to see if you can swim. You always have."

"A naming ceremony. I remember Delbert's. All the gifts, the feast, and dancing into the night. It's the only time my folks allowed us to stay up with the moon." I smiled. "I look forward to mine."

"Now, we will train, and you will apologize to your folks and ask for forgiveness. Promise me you will never run away again. They need to know you are safe." She lifted my chin with a calloused finger.

"I promise. But—"

"*Loot, Kook Yuma Mahooya.* You will respect them, or I will take you to your *Wussa* Erma myself. I am confident she is not who you want to live with."

I frowned. "Yes, ma'am."

"Go pack. And grab a blanket, I'm sure you forgot yours." She stalked off.

"I am packed." I checked my parfleche. Sure enough, I'd forgotten a blanket. I crouched under the entrance of Spupaleena's lodge and plucked a neatly folded wool blanket from the tule bed and stuffed it in my parfleche.

We ate dried salmon, camas cakes, and huckleberries before venturing into the mountains. Spupaleena gathered a few days of supplies and instructed Pekam in what horses to exercise and where we'd be. The air filled with the scent of rain. It did not matter if we had another downpour, I was training with a legend.

I pointed to the sky. "Delbert and I barely got the cows moved yesterday before it rained on us. Rained good and hard." Dark clouds spread across the blue sky. But we rode anyway.

"We rode in the morning and then rested the remainder of the day," Spupaleena said. "Made a plan for future sales. The soldiers are interested in many of our horses because they are strong and fast."

Images of soldiers on her horses paraded across my mind. They covered a lot of ground. Her horses would be a suitable fit–strong with endurance.

We rode south and then west into the mountains, pitching camp by what Spupaleena called Frosted Meadows because when the rest of the land was hot and parched like the desert, this area remained cool and lush. I suspected that night would be cold. I hadn't packed a blanket, thinking I'd be spending my nights in my auntie's lodge next to a warm fire if needed.

We pitched camp by a creek. Birds chirped and squirrels chattered as if welcoming us while we unloaded. It pleased me to be away from my folks' constant nagging. A rustling noise shook nearby brush and captured my attention. Soon a black bear and her cub waddled across the meadow. I jumped to my feet and searched my parfleche for a weapon, realizing I had none. If only I had Pa's rifle. Heck, I could shoot a worm out of a bird's mouth. "There mountain lions in these parts?" I searched the horizon for other beasts.

"*Kewa*. Why?"

I swallowed the lump in my throat. "We have no weapons."

Spupaleena pulled a knife from the legging of her moccasin and held it up. "We have this." She grinned. "Do not worry, *Kook Yuma Mahooya*. We will be safe." She motioned to the sky. "*Koolenchooten* watches out for us."

We set up camp and had a meager meal of jerked venison, baked bitterroot, and serviceberries. My mouth watered at the thought of Mama's fried cabbage with biscuits and gravy. It would have at least stuck to my sides.

We took a short ride around the meadow before the sun sank for the night. We followed the creek a ways before coming to a dam. "Look!" Spupaleena pointed, speaking softly. A beaver floated on the surface, dove into the water, and came up with his paws to his mouth. It looked like he was eating something. Perhaps some sort of vegetation.

"*Sweenompt iss stoonhuh*." I glanced over to Spupaleena and gave her a sly grin.

"*Kewa*, the beaver is handsome. How quickly you learn the language."

"Mama teaches me as she learns from you and your family. I love speaking your language, it's beautiful. And hard. Don't think I'll ever master that deep sound that comes from the back of the throat, but it is fun trying."

"It is. My grandmother taught me to cough loudly and spit out what was deep in my throat when I was a little girl. It worked. My sister and I giggled a lot while practicing."

"What happened to your sister?"

Spupaleena's gaze dropped to the ground. "She died of a broken heart."

I wanted to ask more, but the look on her face suggested I keep my curiosity to myself. So I did.

We watched beaver and his family play in the water and chew on wood before turning back to camp. Once the horses were taken care of and picketed, we reclined on our blankets and stared at the stars. They twinkled dimly in the dusk. Soon, they'd cover the heavens like a shimmering quilt.

"I have a story for you."

I flipped over on my side, leaning on my elbow. "What's it about?"

"Badger."

"What does he do?"

Spupaleena thought a minute. "How do you say

when *Koolenchooten* teaches us a lesson?"

I felt my face blush. "The Lord teaches us humility—Mama calls it eatin' humble pie."

Spupaleena chuckled. "*Kewa*, humility. Elizabeth says we can all use a strong dose of that medicine."

I rolled over on my back, trying to hide my disappointment. I'd hoped for a fun story. Not one aimed at me.

"One time Fox, or *Wha Whelwho*, and coyote lived in the same home. Hunting was poor and they were near starvation. They hunted hard every day, but found no game. Fox decided to leave the territory and hunt elsewhere. Coyote stayed behind. He was stubborn, thinking game would come the next day. But no animals came. Coyote ate insects and leaves which left his belly complaining."

"Could he not catch mice? I thought they were acceptable hunters?"

"I suppose so, but in this story they lacked game. He knew of a camp that had food, but those people hated him. Hunger pangs that hollowed his stomach forced him to scheme until he came up with a plan."

I laughed.

"What is so funny?"

"Coyote's such a greenhorn. He's always getting into trouble. A hard learner, that one."

Spupaleena poked me in the side. "Like someone else I know."

"And someone else I heard stories about." I poked her back, giggling.

"*Kewa,* you are right. I was stubborn, until I was fed a nice big helping of humble cake."

I laughed. "Pie."

"Pie?"

"It's humble pie, not cake, silly."

If it were light outside, I'm sure I could have seen my auntie's face glow the color of hot coals.

"Humble pie. Now, in badger's camp the food was plentiful. Not one belly grumbled. And he was handsome. They called him Sharp Claws. He was a proud warrior and good hunter. Much of the meat he killed he gave to those with little food. Many elders desired him for a son-in-law. But badger did not wish to marry any of their maidens. Like Fox, he thought there would be better choices beyond his village."

I turned to my auntie. "This makes me realize your village is the only one I've ever known. I've not been to Fort Colvile or Pinkney City or Lincoln. I've only been to Kettle Falls to fish, your village, and my cabin. Mama wants me to settle down and marry in a couple of years. With who? Where would I ever find a husband? I don't know anyone, except the boys in your village and they all hate me because I whip them racing." I held back a smile as I thought about the look on their hardened faces last time I won.

Spupaleena reached out and held my hand. "Pray, and *Koolenchooten* will give you the answers."

"I reckon so. But things are lookin' as dim as murky water."

In the shadows of the light, I saw Spupaleena hold a hand over her mouth, shoulders shaking.

I scrunched my nose. "Are you laughing?"

She shook her head.

"Yes. You are!"

She uncovered her mouth and a high-pitched squeal came from her lips. "I am sorry. But this is not the end of the world. If you do not want a husband, why are you worried about finding one?"

Giggles perked inside of me, drowning out my embarrassment, and I found myself joining in the laughter. "I have not a clue."

Once Spupaleena settled down, she continued her story. "One day, when Badger's four sisters went to the river to take their baths, they came upon a pretty woman. She sat on the bank and painted her face with many colors. The sisters favored how she looked. They invited her to their lodge, hoping their brother would take her as his wife. When he came home from hunting, he was pleased she was there. She agreed to marry him, but told him she first had to take meat to her elder folks and needed the help of his sisters."

"Did he agree? Did they go?" My mind whirled with questions. "Was this a trick?"

"Yes, he granted her wish. The next morning, the women carried packs of dried meat to the lodge of the pretty woman. She made the sisters wait outside, as her folks did not like strangers. They brought the meat into the tule-pit dwelling and heard voices. The door-flap opened and Coyote jumped out of the tule-pit lodge. He laughed over the joke he had played on Badger and his sisters, pretending he was the pretty woman."

I gasped. "He didn't. What a cruel creature!"

"*Kewa*, he was always the trickster. The sisters were hot with rage. They ran home and told Badger. He was angry and embarrassed. His people learned what had happened, even though they tried to keep it a secret. A few days later, Badger wanted to take a sweat bath. He went to the pit house and found others already there. They teased him, calling him names. They shamed him for not taking a wife of his own people, saying Badger liked Coyote better. They would not sweat with him."

"The racers call me bad names. I hate it." I turned back on my side, facing my auntie.

"It does hurt," Spupaleena's voice softened, "and even though Badger earned the shame, he turned from the sweat house and went in search of Coyote. He found the crooked animal and chased him out of the territory. Once home, he was proud no more. He humbled himself before all the people and took from among them a wife."

"So you think I should stop racing and take a husband?" I said.

"I think you need to humble yourself and ask *Koolenchooten* for wisdom in choosing the right path. You often skip down the wrong trail, taking a journey on your own, leaving Him behind. Sometimes it is a good journey. Other times it is a hard lesson for you. Perhaps it is time to ask not what is best for only you, but you and your family."

"But you raced at my age. Still do. You had to battle like a warrior to be allowed in, and you made it. Why can't I?"

"Hannah, I caused my father and brother much pain. If I were to do it again, I may not have been so stubborn. *Kewa*, I race, train, have my own herd, but look at the trouble I caused. Pekam almost died."

I rolled over on my other side, my back toward Spupaleena.

"Please pray about this," she said.

I'll pray the Lord allows me to race!

Chapter 4

I woke up shivering, my thoughts running wild while I tossed and turned all morning. Do I quit? Do I keep going? At what cost? Who am I hurting? Delbert doesn't race. It's me and Moonie. When Pekam was badly injured there was an unexpected snow storm in early spring. It's summer. We'd get lightning and thunder. Perhaps a downpour. "No one will get hurt," I whispered. I was certain.

Nature called, so I crept to the bushes. A slight rain last night was enough to soak the ground, my blankets, and skirt. "Blasted!" I'd forgotten a change of clothing. I covered my mouth and leaned around the bushes, peering at Spupaleena's vacant blanket. "Of course she's up."

I took care of my business as quickly as I could and came back to the cracking of a small fire. Spupaleena added pine needles and fir cones. Smoke swirled up as did my prayers.

"Where did you find dry fuel?" I rubbed my hands above the barely visible flames.

Spupaleena cupped her hands and blew on the blue and orange cricket-sized flicker. "I always tuck some away, especially when I can smell rain in the air."

I studied the sky. It looked to be clearing. "Where are

we riding today?" In a few weeks summer storms would pass and blistering heat would singe the earth. I tried to appreciate the dampness while it lingered.

Spupaleena added twigs. "We will ride the hills in this area then head back to the village." She fanned the flames with a slab of bark. "Have you thought about Badger?"

I hunkered close to the fire and dropped pine needles on the struggling fire, hoping my dress would dry before we headed out to ride. "Somewhat."

"And?"

"I'm not giving up. I can't." I braided my hair and tied it off with a thin strip of leather.

Spupaleena strode to her saddle pack and took out dried salmon, bannock, and the rest of the berries. She handed some to me. "I understand how you feel."

I took a bite of salmon and chewed, trying not to gag. Bacon for breakfast I liked. Dried salmon stuck in my throat.

"On our way back, think about your journey. It can be dangerous. I race for different reasons than you. This is the last time you train with me. I won't come between you and your *toom*. She is my family. Your *mistum* saved my life. I love and respect them and will not go against their wishes."

I choked down the salmon and sipped water. "What do I have to do?"

"Everything I say. You fight me once and we are done. You understand?"

"Yes, ma'am." I tossed a handful of berries in my mouth and chewed on her words.

We finished our meal and saddled up. I rode Moonie up and down the creek until Spupaleena was ready. She sat by the fire, head bowed. I said a prayer of my own.

When finished she kicked dirt on the fire and hopped onto her horse. With a somber expression she said, "*Cha hooy-huh.*" She kicked her horse into a trot and headed downstream.

I followed. We rode beside the creek for a bit, trotting in and out of the water. Moonie balked a couple times when we came off higher banks and into the creek. She didn't mind so much if the banks were level with solid sand or dirt. Soft muck made her hesitate.

"That way." Spupaleena nodded to the mountains south of us.

The ground was more grass than rocks, making for a safe place to work horses. We spent most of the morning trotting in and out of trees, crossing the creek in several spots, and jumping over downed logs. Moonie trotted smoothly around the trees and blasted through the water. I felt free. Free of worry. Free of pleasing everyone but me.

Things were going well until the boys showed up. Three Indian boys, quivers slung over their backs and bows in hands. They rode at a walk until they saw us then kicked their horses, picking up speed and war-whooping. They rode straight at us. Moonie danced and skirted sideways.

Spupaleena shouted something at them in Sinyekst. But they kept coming. "Hold your ground!" she hollered at me.

I circled Moonie until she calmed down. They were closing in on us. I stayed close to Spupaleena.

"I think they live over the hill in the San Poel territory. More than likely Okanogans." Spupaleena's mare pricked her ears forward, holding steady.

I studied them as they approached. "Look like tenderfoots to me."

They appeared young, riding seasoned horses. One looked as though still wet behind the ears with his soft face and bright smile. The other two, narrow-eyed with set jaws, tried to act mean and scary. I was not convinced they could frighten a rabbit, although I didn't care much for one of them waving his bow in my face.

Upon reaching us, they circled, chanted, and hollered like coyotes caught in a metal-jawed foot trap. Too bad their lips weren't caught in one of those contraptions. I sneaked a sideways glance at Spupaleena. She glared at the boys as if they were toddlers riding stick ponies.

Straight-faced, Spupaleena sat on her horse and let them show their ill display of manhood. It was short-lived. Two rode off while one hung back. He spoke to Spupaleena. I caught the words, *Hahoolawho* and long ago. Spupaleena's face went dark. With a twisted expression, the boy shouted more words and galloped off.

"What burr was under his saddle?" I shook my head, hoping he'd slide off his horse and hit the ground hard.

She shook her head. "It is not important." She waved me forward. "Come, time to head back to the village."

We rode up a hill and around and down the mountain that led us toward her tule lodge. She instructed me on how to start a race, how to get out in front, how to stay there, and reminded me to ignore insults. She talked about pacing Moonie and when to push her to the end. I asked every question that came to mind, and she answered with wisdom that came with experience and grit.

When we arrived at the twin lakes in the upper valley, we stopped to rest the horses. We sought relief from the heat under a grove of aspen trees. A breeze fluttered their leaves. My face felt like it was melting so I shed my clothing, all but my underclothes, and dove into the cool water. I swam out a bit and turned back. "Come on in!" I splashed water on the sand in front of Spupaleena.

She stood, ripped off her dress, and jumped in bare naked. Her long, dark hair floated on the surface behind her. We splashed and played until goosebumps lined our arms and legs, then dressed and lay on our backs as clouds drift southeast, exposing the hot rays of the sun.

"What did that boy say?" I rubbed the bumps from my arms. "I know it's none of my business, but I've never seen you look so riled. I thought you were gonna pull him off his horse and stomp on him." I let out a hearty snicker. "Reckon he'da deserved it."

Spupaleena nodded, staring past me. After a long moment she spoke. "When I was young and winning all the time, there was a jealous boy who hated me racing because I was a girl. I think he just plain hated me. He tried everything to stop me. One night he snuck into the village and poisoned my horse. I was hurt and angry and rode off by myself on one of the other horses just before dark. Later that night I came back. The village seemed empty and I knew something was wrong. I found my people gathered around my half-dead horse. After pushing my way past the crowd, I came to Smilkameen standing over him." With a hitch in her voice, she nodded. "Her medicine brought him back. When he was strong I raced him again and won. That only made the boy angrier. He was blinded by rage. Then something happened. His face went from evil to gentle. We never spoke about it. Then one day I saw him watching me before a race. It was as if *Koolenchooten* took hold of his heart, stopped it, and restarted it, making a different human."

"Sounds like he tormented you."

"*Kewa*, he did." Spupaleena smiled. "But that was long ago. I have forgiven him. I do not want to hold bitterness close. It eats ones insides. Kills the spirit."

I flung a rock into the lake. "I heard him say Hahoolawho. Was that the boy?"

She nodded. "It was. The one who shouted at me is his son and he threatens revenge."

"Why? You did nothing to him."

"I do not know why. But will pray for him. He is young and foolish."

I leaned against a tree. A loon dove for fish, popping up after some time and several feet away from where it dove in. Its black head, white neck, and black body with white spots reflected in the water. Their coloring and patterns reminded me of a majestic beast, one that exuded honor and respect. Elegance blended in. A single loon wailed a long, mournful call. Its mate responded. Another called, in short, quick yipping sounds. Another joined in. They called to one another until only the sound of the aspen leaves quaked in the breeze. Their calls made me ponder a mate of my own. What would he look like? Would he be brave like Pa? Strong like Jack? Wise like Skumheist? Spupaleena's voice broke into my thoughts.

"When you race, relax your legs so Moonshine relaxes and rides with you. Be ready for anything. Listen to her every movement," Spupaleena said. "Resist the insults or they will distract you."

"But their voices stay in my head. They will not leave me alone." I tossed a rock in the water.

"You must learn to control your thoughts."

I sighed. "Why does Wind Chaser hate me?"

"His anger is not about you. His father is hard on him. His mother died giving birth to his crippled brother. He blames *Koolenchooten* and holds tightly to his grief."

"Grief or not, I have not earned such retribution."

"No. It is best to pray for him…"

I spat in the dust. "Never!"

Spupaleena stared past me for a long time. "When you focus on your horse and what is in front of you, all other voices fade."

"I try…"

"Mmmm," Spupaleena said deep in her throat. "I used to sing songs to my horses. Still do. Songs my *toom* used to sing to me. Before she died."

"What happened to her?" I wasn't sure if she'd answer me or not, but I had to find out. There had to be another deeper reason why Spupaleena threw herself at her horses.

"A mountain lion attacked her." Her voice sounded low and sorrowful as she stirred up old wounds. "My sister and I were young girls. We were in the mountains picking huckleberries. I remember singing and playing. We had wandered off. I could hear *Toom* singing, but could not see her. Everyone was spread out. Winter had been harsh with little food. There was movement in the brush. At first I thought it was a small animal like a rabbit or grouse, but when the hair on the back of my neck stood up, I knew there was danger. I grabbed Mourning Dove's hand and pulled her close. We crept toward our *toom* and saw the mountain lion on top of her. She struggled, kicking and screaming. We yelled and threw rocks at the mountain lion. He ran off, but it was too late. Her neck was shredded, blood trickling from her wounds. The other women and children came running." She swiped a tear from her face. "Mourning Dove did not talk for days."

I swallowed hard. "That must have been a dreadful sight."

"*Kewa.* Mourning Dove was a gentle, loving spirit. Until..."

For the first time in my life, I didn't know what to say. My aunt had been through a lot in her life: watching her mother die, her running off, hurt, my pa finding her bruised and broken. Her sister dying as well as her grandmother and little brother. She'd lost all the people in her life that touched her. I wiped a single tear from my eyes. Blinked back the rest.

"It's time to go." Spupaleena stood.

"I'm sorry—"

"No more talk of sadness. It is bad medicine. It is time to think about your race. Keep your thoughts focused on healing and what you must do to keep ahead and keep the lead."

I swung into the saddle and urged Moonie forward. I opened my mouth to ask some questions, and shut it, allowing the silence to settle my heart. I couldn't get thoughts of Spupaleena's mother's death out of my mind. Bad Medicine. *Lord, help me.*

Chapter 5

It was dusk when we crested the last hill leading to the village. Silhouettes of Sinyekst lodges dotted the flat land that ran along the Columbia River. The closer we came to Spupaleena's lodge, the more in focus the familiar Stetson became. The hitched walk exposed his identity. My heartbeat pounded in my ears.

"I figured you'd be here," Pa said.

I dismounted.

"She is here. And safe. And crotchety as ever." Spupaleena grinned. After unsaddling her horse, she led him away—no doubt to let my father give me a good lickin'.

"Pa—"

"If you're going to hand me a passel full of excuses, don't." He leaned against the corral railing.

I unsaddled Moonie and brushed her down. "There are no excuses." I put her in the corral and slid two poles in place to keep her in.

"What is it going to take to make you listen?"

"I feel the same way." I pinched my arm to keep my tone respectful.

He sighed. "I s'pose you've made your decision. You'll be headed to Montana in a day or two." He ran his fingers over his chin whiskers.

I leaned over the corral rail. "Do you want me to go away?"

He mopped his face with his shirtsleeve. "No, but I reckon it's the only way."

"Way to what? Live like everyone says I should? I really don't have a say? I'm nearly of the marrying age. I'm not a little girl any more, Pa." I spoke just above a whisper.

He chuckled. "That's what your mother and I have been trying to tell you. It's about time to settle down. Consider your future. Life is hard work. Food doesn't land on the table by itself."

I eyed him, looking for weak spots. "Let me race this summer. Then I promise I will consider settling down. Possibly search for a husband. Although I don't know where I'll rope one, living close to nowhere." Crickets chirped in the distance, gratin' on my nerves.

"It's never one more time, one more year."

I scowled.

Pa untied a rawhide bag from his saddle. "Your mama sent a change of clothes and a blanket. There is food in this parfleche, too. We'll stay here for the night and head home at first light. I'll bunk with Skumheist."

"Where are my clothes?"

"In Spupaleena's lodge." He turned and walked away. No hug. No "Everything will work out," like when I was a child. He always made everything okay. Except for now. My empty stomach knotted. His limp more pronounced, he wore a tired expression. The lines etched on his tanned face grew deeper. Gray crowded out sandy brown hair.

"Pa…"

He hobbled toward Skumheist's lodge, not looking back.

I found clean clothes, changed, and nibbled on a biscuit and dried apples. Not ready to talk with anyone, I sat and brushed my hair. Spupaleena entered, took hold of the brush, and worked out the knots. Her strokes were gentle and soothing.

"My *toom* used to brush my hair and braid it for me." She continued to work tangles out of my hair with slow, gentle strokes. "I miss her touch." She took in a deep breath. I felt her smile, her voice attempting to sound chipper. "Your *toom* used to brush my hair when she came to visit. You were a small child back then. When your mother finished braiding my hair, you would pester me until I brushed your hair."

I frowned. "I liked those days. She doesn't brush my hair or Lillian's anymore."

"There can still be times like that, merely different because you are no longer a young child. You are becoming a woman."

"So everyone keeps tellin' me." I fingered the buckskin strip that would tie my braid. "Can you talk to my pa? You know how it feels to want something so badly it hurts. You know how to fight for it against everyone's thoughts and opinions."

She brushed my hair several strokes before answering. "*Loot.* That is between you and your father."

I shoved the brush away. "I need to talk with him." I rushed out of the lodge. I had to apologize.

I trotted to Skumheist's lodge. Pa sat and stared into the crackling fire, a defeated look on his face. His eyes seemed tired. Skumheist sat across from him, doing most of the talking and using a lot of hand gestures. Pa grunted and nodded every so often. I crept close, hearing my name.

Skumheist talked about his battle with his daughter and her strong will when she was my age. How she and I were alike. How battling our strong minds kept us separated. He talked of his regrets and unwillingness to allow her to race in the beginning. How he should have supported her. In the end, she ran from him. He talked about how she drew Pekam into racing. How he resisted his children's desires, trying to make them do things they were not interested in. He talked about changing times and how resistance causes tears and broken hearts and rebellion.

He instructed my father to choose his decisions only after much prayer. That Pa could either support me and keep me close and safe, or send me far away and not know how or what I was doing. If I was determined to race here, I'd find a way to race in Montana.

I set my mouth. And I would.

Pa nodded. "I will consider all you have said, my friend. I agree, our daughters are greatly alike. I don't want to see her get hurt. I don't want her to keep running away and neither does Elizabeth." He shook his head. "She's always been a spitfire."

"She has much talent. Support her and she will grow stronger and wiser as my daughter has. Believe in her and she will keep safe. *Koolenchooten* will guide her."

"You're right. The Lord will guide her." He rubbed the back of his neck. "I pray she follows. Pray for us as I pray for wisdom and strength."

"I have been praying for you for many years. I will continue."

They stared at the fire, saying nothing more.

I crept backward, hoping the crickets would drown out any sound my boots made while leaves and twigs crackled under my feet. When I knew I was out of sight and sound, I turned and rushed to Spupaleena's lodge. It was empty. I lay on my tule mat and covered up with the blanket Pa gave me. Even though my eyes grew tired, my mind raced.

The next morning, I rose to the smell of bacon and flapjacks. "Pa must be cookin'."

Spupaleena shoved a basket of duck eggs in my hands. "Give these to him."

I walked as fast as I could without breaking any eggs, cradling the basket in my arms. Then slowed, remembering he didn't know I had listened in on their conversation the previous night. I replaced my smile with a somber look. I shook my head, knowing that wouldn't do. It'd be too obvious. So I thought about the stern talkin' to I got last night. And Pa frettin' about my safety. I put on a solemn expression and dragged my feet to the fire like wounded bird. I sat on a log with the basket in my lap. "Need help?"

He pointed to the coffee pot. "Yeah, pour me a cup, please."

I did so. Then poured me one, too. I took a sip and winced. Pa snickered. "If I have to drink this bitter coffee to ripen into womanhood, I'll stay young." I set my cup aside and handed him the eggs.

Pa set a second pan on a rock by the fire, added lard, and cracked an egg. It sizzled. He cracked more, until a half dozen were bubbling. He forked bacon and flipped flapjacks. He worked the food like one of the cooks on a cattle drive I'd read about in some of my books. He handed me a metal spatula and told me to watch the eggs.

"When are we leaving?" I tried not to sound overly gloomy. Enough to make it believable.

Pa smiled. He forked the bacon and slid brown flapjacks on a wooden plate he'd made for Sumheist. Took a sip of coffee.

I sighed and stared thoughtlessly at the sky. "Pa, I'm sorry."

He flipped more flapjacks. "I know you heard us talkin' last night." Pa glanced at me. "I saw you sneak away."

I blushed, turning my face away.

"Skumheist and I had quite the talk. I'm not certain how much you heard."

I opened my mouth to tell him, then snapped my lips shut, pressing them tightly together.

He grinned at me. "What's that look for?"

"What look?" I gave him a small smile. I flipped the eggs, sending bits all over the inside of the cast iron skillet.

He motioned to the chaos. "You fryin' or scramblin' those?"

"Frying." I patted them with the spatula.

Pa placed bacon next to the flapjacks and set the pan in the dirt.

"Smells familiar." Pekam sniffed the air. He sat on a log across from me and glanced in the pan. "You frying those or scrambling them?"

Pa laughed.

I grunted. "Fryin'…just how you like 'em—all mixed up." I lobbed a rock at him.

Pekam dodged it. "If you cook like you throw, we are all in trouble." He tossed the rock in the skillet and it landed on an egg. "I will eat that one." He held out his hands.

"You certainly will." I slapped his hands with the spatula.

Spupaleena and Skumheist wandered over and sat down. After a quick prayer over the food, I ate. They ate and teased me about my cooking. When the food had disappeared and the fun died down, the mood turned serious. I glanced around. All eyes were pinned on me. I turned my attention to the fire, poking it with a stick. I was certain he'd changed his mind, and I was headed for Montana. My mind spun, planning escape routes.

Pa cleared his throat. "I've changed my mind."

I knew it! I stopped poking charred wood and looked at him, trying to keep a somber face. I stole glances at Skumheist, Spupaleena, and Pekam. Skumheist's expression was as solid as a wolf stalking a meal. Pekam's eyes dazzled in the firelight. Spupaleena's were glued to her horses, as usual. I presumed she was brooding over the next horse sale, or her next race, or thanking the Lord I was leaving.

I dragged my focus back to Pa. His eyes were still pinned on me. "You will remain here and train with Spupaleena."

I gasped, jumping to me feet to embrace him, but he stopped me with his hand. "There are rules."

I eased my backside onto the log, my gaze drifting to Spupaleena. Straight-faced, she arched a brow at me. She didn't look like she was thrilled about the new arrangement. She'd made it clear—one time—she never went back on her word. I picked up my fire-poking stick and drew circles in the dirt. My mind shifted to rules. There were always rules. Rules for riding. Rules for dress.

Rules for conduct. Rules for marriage—what type of suitor. What he'd do to make a life for us. How many children and what to name them. It exhausted me. "All right." It's all I could choke out and remain fairly ladylike.

"You will need to listen to everything Spupaleena tells you. She's kindly agreed to let you stay. One of us will make weekly visits to check on you. You will help out with chores around the village when you are not riding."

"Who is 'one of us'?" I glanced around the circle.

"Me, your mama, Delbert, Jack." He frowned at the fire stick. "And anyone else I can drum up."

I tossed the stick in the fire. "Yes, sir."

"Everything will be fine. The Lord will provide and protect." Pa swallowed, looking like he was trying to convince himself of the truth in his own words.

"You tryin' to convince me or yourself?" I slapped a hand over my mouth.

Pa scowled at me. "I reckon both of us. And you'll keep up with your Bible readin', ya hear?"

I scrunched my nose. "But I didn't bring it."

"I figured not." Pa reached into this saddle bag and handed me my Bible. "You're gonna have to learn to pack better'n you did to survive the wilderness."

My face heated.

Everyone laughed.

"She will obey me," Spupaleena said with narrow eyes and a sloppy grin. "If she doesn't, Pekam is willing to escort her to Montana. I'm confident *Wussa* Erma would be happy to have her."

My eyes darted to my uncle. He smiled and nodded.

Pa packed up and headed for home. As he disappeared through the trees, it occurred to me how blessed I truly was. I thanked the Lord for making Pa see things my way.

I turned to ask Spupaleena when we were gonna ride, but found Pekam. He held out a dozen deer bladders to me. "Fill these up. Then you can water Moonie and picket her to eat. Then you can—"

I ripped the bladders out of Pekam's hands and stomped to the river.

Chapter 6

"Do not cross my sister." Pekam leaned against the corral, watching me saddle Moonie.

"Don't reckon I will."

"I mean it. I did. Once." He smiled, poking a blade of grass in his mouth. One waist-long braid draped over his shoulder and hung over the right side of his bare, tan chest. The other hid behind him. His worn leggings needed mending and one toe peeked out of a moccasin.

His tattered buckskin distracted me. "I see your clothes are in need of repair."

He wiggled a toe. "You can fix them tonight. I'll add it to your list."

I grimaced. In no way had I offered my services. I swallowed bits of pride with hot saliva, telling myself to keep my mouth shut. "What happened when you disobeyed Auntie?"

He laughed. "I had chores coming out of my ears for many suns."

I arched a brow. "How many?"

"I stopped counting after fifty."

I knew at that moment there was no room for blunder. The thought of being escorted to Montana by anyone gave me a bitter taste in my mouth. Especially

Uncle Pekam. I knew he'd chide me every step. Tellin' me I shoulda listened. Shoulda done everything Spupaleena told me to do. He would've reminded me how I'd blow my chance of learning from the finest.

Truth was, Spupaleena was the finest. And not just in Washington Territory. Jack said folks talked about her throughout the west. I set my shoulders. *Keep your mouth shut and do what you're told, Hannah Gardner.* After I filled bladders with water, cared for Moonie, washed horse and human blankets and hung them to dry over corral poles, and set berries out to dry, Spupaleena came for me. My chores had taken several hours. My skin and clothing were dirt-covered, my muscles and neck ached, and sweat ran down my back like waterfalls.

Spupaleena studied my dirt-covered self and shook her head. "Time to ride."

"I'll run to the river and wash off—"

"*Chahooyhuh!* No time."

I grumped and followed her to Moonie's corral. After saddling my horse, I led her to Spupaleena. She laced up her moccasins, wound them around her calf, and tied them below the knee. She slipped a small bone knife in her right legging. "You ready?"

Dry-mouthed, I nodded. "Let me slip on Delbert's britches."

She reached in a buckskin bag hanging from the corral post and tossed me a pair of tattered leggings. "Put these on."

I peeked around, seeing no one. I lifted my skirt and slipped them on over my drawers and stockings.

Spupaleena motioned to my head. "Where is your hat?"

I glanced over my shoulder. It hung off the corral post. I grabbed it, snugged it down over my eyes, and mounted.

Heavy as they were, the leggings stuck me to the saddle. I circled Moonie around at a trot, waiting for Spupaleena. Ears swiveling back and forth, she seemed a tad spooky. I eyed the timberline, but didn't see anything out of order. She may have smelled a mountain lion or bear farther out. A shiver ran down my back. As long as they didn't bother me, I didn't care where they roamed.

Spupaleena whistled to me and we rode north.

"Pekam will catch up to us. He has a few chores to finish."

I smiled, thinking he might still be in trouble. "Hard learner, I 'spect."

"What?"

I gave her a fake cough. "What are we doing first?" I tried not to sound overly eager.

Spupaleena pointed toward smaller mountains and hills is the distance. "Working the fat off Moonshine."

As we rode along, my mind drifted to racing. I saw myself winning piled-high loot. The kind Spupaleena used to win: blankets, pots and pans, saddles, beads, food. I thought about what I'd do with it all. Save some, give some to Lillian for her dowry, let Delbert pick though leftovers.

While I still daydreamed, Pekam caught up with us. A few miles farther we began to climb the first mountain. Half way up, sweat dripped off Moonie. Her sides heaved. I'd thought she was well conditioned—apparently not enough. We rested in the shade of fir trees and let her and the other horses catch their breaths. A gentle breeze, enough to offer a break from rising heat, blew stray hairs in my face. I combed them under my hat.

"Most of the women are up here picking berries. If you make it to the top, we can stop and gather some too. Up ahead is a nice pond." Spupaleena pointed up a steep hill. She pointed to sweat rolling off my horse's flanks. "When Moonie is ready."

I gulped. "Up that?"

Pekam frowned. "Better get used to it. If you want to race with the men, you and Moonie need to be able to climb at least three hills this steep." He handed me a bladder of water.

"How long do I have?" I took a long swallow.

"You have plenty of time," Spupaleena said. "You will not race until I say you are ready." She scowled at Pekam.

Pekam grinned at his sister. "That is right. I keep forgetting you are, as Jack tells us, the trail boss."

"What does that make you, Uncle?" I said with a smile.

Spupaleena wiggled his braid. "My little doggie."

-We all laughed.

"Best get goin'." I pinned my focus uphill and kicked Moonie into a trot. But as steep as the hill was, she broke into a steady walk and crept her way up. I dropped my reins low and let her pick her way uphill. I rubbed her neck and hummed.

Dead branches and dried leaves cracked under horses' hooves as we weaved in and out of trees. I searched for huckleberry patches. There weren't any close to our cabin and for me, they were a delicacy.

I followed Spupaleena while Pekam flanked me when the trail narrowed. My Indian relatives kept me in the center, as if needing protection, or like a prisoner going to my hanging. Nevertheless, I kept my mouth shut. Thankfully in some spots we fanned out and I could relax.

Then it hit me. What if all this was part of a bigger plan to get me to crawl home on my own? *Swindlers!* What had I agreed to? Only one race? Not the entire summer? Hard work with little free time. I never did clarify this plan Pa conjured up 'cause I was too excited about stayin'. Narrow eyed, I studied my aunt and uncle when we'd come on a flat spot. We let the horses rest. I rode away from them, pretending I needed to relive myself. Instead, I made a pact with Moonshine to not let them get the best of me. If Spupaleena could do this at my age, so could I. I'd prove myself. One way or another. I went ahead and took care of my business, not knowing when we'd stop again, still fuming, and not then made my way back to my sidewindin' relatives.

We headed back down the trail. While my mind whirled, a branch struck my cheek, nearly knocking me out of the saddle. It was as though the Lord Almighty reached down from heaven and smacked me, stating enough was enough. My fingers glided over the welts. I winced from the sting. I was still rubbing my cheek when I stopped in front of Spupaleena. Opened mouthed, she stared at me.

Pekam shook his head. "What happened?"

"I…I…" I put my hand down.

"Were you daydreaming again?" Spupaleena said.

Pekam reached for me. "Looks like you sliced your face with a knife."

I blocked his hand. Then reached up, touching warm, thick fluid. Red smeared my fingers. I mopped at it with my shirtsleeve. "I'm fine."

Spupaleena stared at me for a moment. "We need to keep going." She twirled her horse around and sped away.

This time she rode closer to Pekam and I trailed behind. They spoke softly, more than likely plotting how to make things rougher on me. I lifted my chin and hummed to Moonie, focusing on what was in front of us.

After we'd ridden a few more miles we crested the top of the mountain. Several miles of mountains, streams, and a valley spread out in front of us. As did raging clouds that crowded out blue sky. A sweet, unusual scent caught my attention. I turned my nose in different directions and sniffed until I found the source of the addicting smell on a hill bank. To my left was a bush with shiny, thick leaves. I leaned over and picked off a few and stuck them against my nostrils. Its thick, sweet fragrance caught me off guard. I inhaled again. Then picked a few more and put them in my skirt pocket, leaving one out to enjoy. "What is this called?"

Pekam picked a leaf and sniffed it. "We call it *gwigwnlhp*. Your father calls it buckbrush, because deer love to eat it, or so he says."

Spupaleena plucked a leaf from the small brush and studied it. "We boil leaves in water and use it for broken bones and to purify our blood. It is used on burns, on a baby's red bottom, in our hair, before a sweat. We mix it with sap and use it for cuts and other wounds." She pointed to my face. "Use some on your wound tonight."

I fingered the leaf. "Does my mother know about this?"

"She has used it on you many times." Spupaleena took a pouch from around her neck and lobbed it to me. "Put some of this salve on your cheek for now."

I scooped some out with my finger and sniffed. Its strong scent made me wince. I smeared a little on my cut and pitched the pouch back to my aunt.

Spupaleena hung the pouch back around her neck. "There is a creek close by. We can rest our horses and get a drink there before moving on."

Most of the day had passed. I wondered when we'd head back. Or if we were gonna remain on top of the mountain for the night. With a storm comin', I prayed they planned to head back soon. We rode a short distance to a thin creek. I dismounted and gulped icy water until my head hurt. Pekam and Spupaleena laughed. They sipped theirs while I held my head in my hands. We nestled in the shade of trees near a patch of ferns. I fingered its lacy limbs until my headache subsided. "Do we have anything to eat?"

"Did you not bring food?" Pekam said.

I frowned. "No." *Part of the test.*

"Perhaps you did." He ambled to the parfleche bag strapped to the back of my saddle, slid out a pouch, and flung it at me.

I opened it and took out some dried salmon. Clever to have hidden it with me. I'd have to look and see what else he'd snuck in my bag. What I wanted was Mama's cooking. The main food the Indians ate consisted of dried salmon, wild carrots and onions, berries, dried small game, cooked camas and bannock. I wanted her fried cabbage, baked beans, beef steaks, fresh milk, butter, dried apples, fried chicken, stew, bacon, eggs. My stomach growled as I continued the list in my head. I reminded myself there was no room for complaining. *Eat it. Be thankful. Remain here.* I choked down a bite.

"What's next?" I gave a tired smile.

Spupaleena glanced at Pekam. "Follow us. We will ride farther, then circle around and head back. I do not want your horse to fall down because she is tired."

"Moonie will be fine." I glanced at her weary eyes, nose inches from the ground, not really believing she would be.

"The storm is close. We need to go back." Spupaleena stood.

I peered at the black clouds hovering above us. "Will we camp one day? Soon? Like you and Mama used to?"

Spupaleena put out a hand and helped me to my feet. "We will."

"If you wait for a couple days I can go along. I promised Father I would help him dig out his new canoe while our cousin is away," Pekam said.

"Girls only." Spupaleena said. She looked at Pekam's pouty face. "Sorry."

I clapped my hands. *Less work, more riding!*

Chapter 7

Thunder ripped through the mountains. Pekam's colt spooked and bolted downhill.

"Stay close to me!" Spupaleena pointed to her side.

I nodded. A ripple ran though Moonshine's body as lightning split the sky and thunder cracked the air. Her nose stuck close to Spupaleena's mare's rump. I wished I'd paid better attention to the weather. Pa told me how important knowing the horizon was—especially in the mountains. Too late now. Rain dumped on us, soaking our clothes.

Pekam's back disappeared behind a curtain of rain. Spupaleena and I moved forward at a slow trot. I ducked branches. Moonie tripped over debris here and there, but we made it down the first hill. A clearing came into view.

"We have no choice but to ride across the open grass," Spupaleena shouted. She waved me forward.

"Isn't there any way around it?" I searched the tree line, blinking back raindrops.

Spupaleena examined the black sky. "No, we don't have time. The storm is already on top of us."

"But—" I jumped as the next roll of thunder cracked over the mountain tops. "Let's hunker down under the trees and wait out the storm."

"We have to go now." Spupaleena kicked her horse into a gallop.

I circled Moonie around a few times. It was dangerous to ride in the clearing. She reared and bolted forward, chasing after them. As she lurched forward, my fingers instinctively reached for the saddle horn. My hip pitched to the right, but I was able to regain my balance and sit square in the saddle. I reined her back toward the trees. She jumped and reared, attempting to follow Spupaleena's horse. More lightning strikes illuminated the sky and thunder came within a few seconds. I held on tight, praying we wouldn't get struck before we were under shelter. Water pelted my face. I tugged my Stetson as far down as I could and still be able to see. I crouched low, letting Moonie choose her path.

More lightning struck around us and my brain told me to rein in my mare—duck and hide—but my legs kicked her. Moonie spun around and ran faster than a jackrabbit toward the path Spupaleena had taken. I felt vulnerable out in the open with no shelter. We were now the tallest objects in the middle of the clearing and my hat was not the type of shelter I needed. My fingers clung to the reins. I could only count on Moonie to know the way back as Pekam and Spupaleena were long gone. I kicked and prayed, and kicked and prayed, screaming for Spupaleena to wait. My fingers clutched the reins so tight they ached. I shivered from the cold and fright.

Then I felt my mare slide on the slick grass.

We were going down and there was nothing I could do. I stuck my arm out to brace against the fall, and then pulled it back not wanting to mend a broken arm. Her right side collapsed, taking me with her. It all happened so fast. I clutched the saddle horn, trying to keep my head from bouncing off the ground. My right shoulder slammed against the hard ground. I heard the crack and moaned. Felt dizzy. Confused. Was it lightning? Am I struck? I wiggled my fingers and toes.

My head hurt. "Moonie?" With blurred vision, I fumbled around until my fingers ran down her neck. She was still, eyes closed. I lay back and cried before everything went black.

Voices arguing outside Spupaleena's lodge aroused me. How many days had I been out? I blinked open my eyes, squinting against low light. I pressed a hand against my pounding head. Then covered my eyes with a blanket.

"She is going back," Spupaleena said in a hushed voice. "No more."

Pekam's sigh was loud enough for me to hear. "Remember when I was thirteen suns. All I could think about was riding. She is like us. Eager. Strong. Determined."

"Foolish. She will not obey. If she would have kept up with me, this would not have happened." Spupaleena shook a finger in the air. "Look at what our racing did to *Mistum*. And you were hurt. I cannot let this happen to Hannah, too."

"I'm fine. I healed and so will she. We can add chores—"

"No! You will escort her home in the morning, or when she is up to it. Or I will. We all agreed to Phillip's plan. We must keep our word. Keep her safe."

"Smilkameen will heal her."

"She does not need healed on the outside like she

does on the inside. In her heart. There is no medicine for stubbornness and disobedience. Her attitude is the danger. She is careless. You at least obeyed."

"That is why she needs to have her time filled with chores. Hard ones. She can work when we are not training. It made me responsible."

Spupaleena grunted. "You are not what I call responsible, brother."

I heard footsteps pacing and reckoned it had to be Pekam.

"You are just scared she will die like our little brother. You still blame yourself for his death because you were the one watching him by the river when he fell in. She will not die. She is a strong rider." Pekam's voice softened. "His drowning was not your fault, sister. Fear makes your thoughts and mood swirl like a bad windstorm."

Horses whinnied in the distance. *Where is Moonie? They didn't mention her. Is she dead?* With a heavy heart I prayed, tears streaming down my cheeks. I curled into a ball and buried my face in my hands. "She can't be dead!" Spupaleena's voice broke into my fitful sobs.

"She can stay." There was a sigh. "You are right. I have been short tempered with her. It is because I am scared. I love her like family," Spupaleena sighed, "she needs to obey to stay safe. That will be your job."

I lifted my face. "I can stay?"

Hands clapped one time. I assumed it was Pekam.

I dried my tears. His praise shooed away lingering fear and doubt.

"*Host,* good, she will be fine. You will see."

Rapid footsteps came near. The flap of the lodge

swished open.

Cold, rough hands rolled me onto my back and felt my neck and cheeks. I opened my eyes enough to get a glimpse of the grumpy healer and swatted at her. She spoke sharply at me and continued her examination. The legend was the only time anyone had seen her laugh was when Spupaleena pulled her horse out because he came up lame allowing Pekam beat all the men. Since then, the only person she'd favored was my uncle.

I relaxed as she made her medicine. I grunted, coughed from the pain, and as a diversion thought about the meaning of her name—swan. I would have called her skunk. Or gopher. Or mule. Anything but a name implying grace and beauty. Her body was short and squatty and a constant scowl rode her face.

I peeked at her through lowered lashes, pointed to my head, and told how much it hurt in Sinyekst the best I could. She grunted, spreading herbs on a leaf and mixing them with some form of liquid that resembled sap. She motioned for me to sit up. I shook my head, wincing at the pain.

She motioned again, saying, "*Kukneeya,*" with a stern voice.

Knowing that word meant "listen to me now," I sat up and sipped the bitter brew. My lips puckered and a *zing* ran through my jaws. My face heated—I was certain as red as Indian Paint Brush. I wanted to spit it out. More than that, I wanted the pounding in my head to stop, so I swallowed and growled the rancid taste away. Handing the leaf back to her, I swear I witnessed the form of a smile trying to burst forth at my suffering. *Decrepit skunk!*

"I need to talk to Spupaleena."

She shook her head.

"I need to find out if Moonie is alive."

She stared at me with a blank expression on her face.

"Please." I moaned, laying back on my tule-mat. "I know you understand me!"

"*Uks kawup oalth host.*"

"Moonie, she's fine? Where is she?" I tried to rise, but Smilkameen pushed me back down and motioned for me to stay.

The healer sprinkled the same herb on fresh leaves, added the sticky substance, and pressed them against the cuts on my arms and legs. One on my neck. I didn't much like her leaning over me, breathing her cantankerous demeanor over my body.

"Much obliged," I mumbled. My eyes grew heavy. The pain in my head drifted away. All I needed now was my mama's soft touch and the quilt she made me snug against my chin.

Pekam burst in. "Hannah, you awake?"

I peered through slits. "Uh-huh."

"It is time to ride." He took one look at me and knelt down.

I groaned, placing an arm over my forehead.

Pekam gave me a questioning look. "As soon as you can get around. In a day or two."

Smilkameen grunted, holding a leaf over a cut on my leg. Pekam's eyes pleaded with her. She scowled at him, shaking her head.

"Maybe more," he said.

I grabbed his arm. "How's Moonie? Where is she?"

Smilkameen motioned for Pekam to leave.

Pekam walked to the flap door, peered over his shoulder at me, and went outside.

Why didn't he answer me about my mare? I stared at the cedar baskets and buckskin pouches hanging from the sides of the lodge. *Is she all right?* With heaviness, my eyes closed.

CHAPTER 8

Three days later I stood sturdy on my feet, the pain in my head now a dull ache. The bitter taste of Smilkameen's tea lingered in my mouth. Nothing I ate washed it away. I popped a fourth handful of huckleberries in my mouth and let the juice float on my tongue. I rubbed my purple hands on my skirt, trying to rid them of the stickiness, tied my red neckerchief around my neck, and went in search of Moonie, still a might disgruntled no one took account for her well-being.

Spupaleena shot me a sideways glance. "How is your head?" She continued to brush her horse.

"Better. I don't know what that bitter-tasting tea's made of, but it seems to be working." I found a bladder of water and took a long swallow.

"Smilkameen's medicine is strong but it always heals." Spupaleena dropped the brush and untied her horse. "You ready for your first chore?"

"Well…I…um…I thought we were riding?"

"I am riding. You will ride when I think you are ready."

"When will that be?"

"When I say." Spupaleena slipped a bit in her mare's mouth. Her father had traded furs for the bit with one of the Hudson Bay Company workers when he came to terms with his daughter's determination to race.

I rolled dirt around with the toe of my tattered boot.

"You hit your head and it put you to sleep. It may take more time to heal." She studied me. "And do not lie about the pain."

There was no sense arguing with her. I stared at a deep cut on Moonie's chest. A hand-sized patch of hide was missing. My jaw tightened. She shuffled around the corral like an old man beaten down by years of hard work on harsh land. Her head hung low.

"Brush those horses." Spupaleena pointed to a large herd shaded by a tree line across the meadow. "Then take them one by one to get a drink in the river." She handed me a rope halter.

I counted twenty head, not including the foals sprawled out in the grass. "How will I catch them all?"

"As your *toom* says, use your imagination." Spupaleena tossed the brush in a basket. "But first, help Smilkameen with Moonie. As you can see she has many deep wounds."

I turned my attention to the loose horses. "That'll be like ropin' grasshoppers." I took the halter, staring at my mare in the adjoining corral.

"Watch for the happy healer. She will check on you before gathering more medicine." Spupaleena bridled her colt. "*Ninawees*." She swung up on her horse and trotted away.

I grunted. "Happy healer." I dragged my feet to the corral and went inside. Moonshine whickered at me. I rubbed her neck. Two legs were wrapped with doeskin strips. My eyes pooled with tears. I choked them down. "I'm sorry, Moonie. I'm so sorry." I picked up a handful of grass and offered it to her. When she turned her nose away, I sobbed and buried my head in her mane and wept.

"No time to cry." The man's deep voice was filled with compassion.

I dried my tears, picked up a brush, and started in on her back with soft, lazy strokes.

Skumheist lumbered to the other side of Moonie, a frown across his face. "You should be on your way to visit your *wussa*."

I peered at the ground, fighting back tears. "Reckon I should be."

"My son is filled with wisdom." He smiled and walked off.

His declaration baffled me. He'd always been a man of peace and reason. But what I couldn't figure was why he supported me when he was so against racing. He'd surrendered to his own children's stubbornness, and I understood that, but why me? I shrugged. "I suppose tears won't heal your wounds, will they, girl?" Moonie dropped her head as I brushed her body.

I helped Smilkameen change her wrapping with fresh herbs then peeled the rope from the corral post and headed to the tree line.

The loose horses' heads jerked up and the foals sprang to their feet searching for their mothers as I approached. One snorted—more than likely the lead mare. I stopped and knelt on one leg, head down. I figured if they didn't think I was coming to catch 'em, they'd go 'bout their business. I figured wrong. Still hunkered down, the snorty lead ushered the other ones south at a good clip. I stood, hands on hips. After stomping a leg and kicking twigs and pinecones, I took several deep breaths and waited to see where they might have been fixin' to settle and return to grazing. Except they weren't stopping. If fact, they picked up speed. With Moonie injured, there was no chance of catching them.

Skumheist sat in the shade, watching the fiasco. I stomped over to him, out of breath and steaming mad. He grinned at me, although I didn't take it as a "Howdy" kinda declaration. He waved bugs from his face and looked up at me.

I cleared my throat then glanced at the horses, stirrin' up nerve. "You gotta pony I can borrow to chase that bunch?"

He examined the runaways and then turned to me. "*Loot*." He fingered a two-inch wooden canoe in this hand. It looked as though it was almost finished.

"None at all?" The herd disappear around a bend.

He shook his head.

I sighed. "I really messed things up." I sank to the ground and rubbed my temples.

He worked on the canoe, smoothing the rough parts with the edge of his bone knife blade.

"Think I'll ever learn?"

He nodded, peeling another layer of wood from the toy. "Slow down. Think like a horse. Look around and use what you see." He ran a finger over the canoe. "This toy does not take long to make. But the ones that carry us up the Columbia take many suns. We work slowly and carve out pieces every day. With two or more working, it goes by faster."

A handful of young boys played a game with a buckskin ball and sticks with long, shallow baskets on the end of each one. They tossed the ball in the air to another player and chased after them. "Are you saying I need help?"

He examined both sides of the canoe, running a finger over the wood.

I frowned. "Are you suggesting I convince those boys to help me?"

Skumheist grinned. "You learn quickly." He handed me the tiny canoe. "Let this remind you to think on things. Let it guide your thoughts the same way it glides on the water and carries us upriver. It may be at a slower pace, but it carries us to where we need to go. It holds power." He peered up at the cloudy sky. "Ask *Koolenchooten* for wisdom."

I slid off my Stetson and mopped my brow with my shirtsleeve.

"Do ya really think they'll help me?"

"Ask." He rose and ambled back to the village.

I settled my hat back on my sweaty head and lazily rose to my feet. After dousing my head in the river and drinking left-over willow tea, I managed to round up five of the boys playing the stick game. My Sinyekst was decent enough to share my predicament. The boys gathered Indian hemp ropes—appearing eager to show this prairie girl a thing or two. I lifted my chin, and my skirt, and lead the way.

The horses hadn't traveled as far as I'd thought. One boy, the oldest I 'spect, motioned for us to circle the herd. We did, hunkering down in tall grass. We observed them for a short while. Then the leader crept up to a lone mare and slipped a rope around her neck. The other four followed suit. I found a nice mare and went to put a rope around her neck, but found one hand empty and the other clutching the toy canoe. The boys stared at me. They laughed and walked off with the rest of the herd following them. I took up the drag—empty handed and eating their dust. I reckoned I deserved it. Never took the time to fetch a rope as I was too worried about lookin' like a fool.

I fingered my canoe. *Slow down. Pray.* I envisioned myself in a full-sized canoe, gliding across smooth water. Sun in my face and the smell of salmon surrounding me. The Lord right there beside me, us talking like old comrades. Then in my mind I saw a storm swirling overhead. The water turned choppy. I screamed and reached for the Lord but he was gone. The canoe sank and I went with it.

The boys turned around and laughed, bringing me back to the present. With a scowl on my face, I followed the horses to the edge of the village. One of the boys, one with a hint of compassion spread over his face and dancing eyes, handed me a rope. I slipped the canoe into my skirt pocket. Dancing Eyes glanced at Skumheist who sat in the bottom of his canoe. Dancing Eyes nodded, and walked off. Skumheist picked up a scraping tool and proceeded to dig out more of his canoe.

Not certain what that exchange was all about, I lifted my chin, looked straight ahead, and caught the closest horse. I walked her to the edge of the sand and shed my boots and stockings, then lifted my skirt and tied the loose fabric in a knot at my waist.

The mare sniffed the water and inched in. After pawing several times, splashing her legs and chest, she drank. Eyes half-mast, her head came up, water dripping from her muzzle. I dipped my hands and took a sip. Then took the neckerchief from around my neck, swirled it around in the river, and tied it back on. I poured water over my head with my hat and squealed from the cold.

The mare jumped back and I lost my balance, falling into the water. The mare bolted and made her way back to the herd, lead rope dragging in the dirt.

The boys laughed from the bank. Dancing Eyes slid the rope off, put it on a different horse, and led her to me. The others teased him for being so soft-hearted. He handed me the rope with a big smile. "Much obliged." I felt like walking into the water and drowning my embarrassment.

He jogged back to the others. They war-whooped as they ran back toward the village.

Heat rose up my neck. "Ornery mules." I let the horse drink as I pondered ways to get back at those sidewinders. While walking the mare back, I thought about Dancing Eyes. I'd have to consider him for marriage. His generosity alone made him the kind of man Pa would approve of. Perhaps if I made an effort to find a suitable husband, Mama might let me stay.

With my thoughts fixated on hunting for a husband, it wasn't long before I noticed all the horses stood in the water. Spupaleena's older red stallion was beside me. He allowed me to briefly stroke his neck before spinning around in the ankle-deep water and galloping away. The mare I held jerked the rope out of my grip and tore off, taking the herd with her. I sank my rope-burned hands into the water.

The younger stallion snorted at me. Pawed the ground and shook his head as if in warning. I stood as tall and straight as a tamarack trunk and strode toward him, eyes on his chest. He reared up, coming down hard. I paused. Dropped my gaze to the ground and turned a shoulder to him. He dropped his head in submission. I took a step closer, chin to my chest, hand out. He whinnied and sped off as fast as a chipmunk after a pine nut.

I marched straight past those boys as they cackled, following me. They must have watched the whole thing from behind trees like coyotes. They teased me until the herd came into view. I crossed Dancing Eyes off my list. The leader motioned for the others to circle the horses, same as before. Mad as a wet hen, I knelt in the grass. He quickly caught the same mare and handed her to me. I winced from the rough hemp on my skinned palms. He then caught the young stallion and strode by, a smirk riding his face.

I dropped the mare's rope and stole the stallion's lead right out of the boy's hand. Something he hadn't counted on! Frankly, something I hadn't planned. Startled, the young stallion twirled and reared. I hung on with sheer will to win back my pride, shredding my palms. Then without a second thought, I hoisted myself on his back and ran him right into the river, skirt flapping in the wind. The boys caught up to me, standing at the river's edge. Mouths agape, not one word was said. Who was laughing now!

Chapter 9

My nose under Moonie, Smilkameen had me rub herbal salve on a few belly scratches. I had no idea how she acquired so many. They were not deep, but deep enough to consider infection if not treated. Because of the rain, no one saw us fall. She must have tumbled over sharp rocks and sticks. I couldn't recall what the ground looked like. Everything was a blur. I placed a pinch of salve in a leaf and slid it into the buckskin pouch I'd made the previous night. Then slid my canoe in with it and placed the pouch around my neck. I rubbed extra salve onto my rope burned palms.

While treating my mare, my mind drifted back to the healer and her name—Swan. A short neck peeked out of her buckskin dress. Ample curves stretched the animal hide. Dark braids dropped down her back, tempting me to use them to tie her up to a corral post and have the village kids come and tickle her until she was forced to giggle. Nothin' but a frown covered that scrunched-up face. No how was that woman close to resembling a swan—of any kind—with a slender, arched neck and slim body. Two things they did have in common: beady eyes and long beaks. One graceful, the other cantankerous. I'd always wondered what had hardened her like rawhide.

She handed me fresh buckskin strips and pointed to Moonie's legs. I laid them over one of the corral poles. She then sprinkled herbs in leaves cupped in my hands. I nodded and got to work changing the dressings on a hind leg. I unwrapped the soiled bandage and turned my head to the side when the foul stench hit my nose. Green goop oozed from the wound. Smilkameen mumbled harsh words in Sinyekst and wobbled away. Something awful must have happened to the old woman to make her behave that way. I rinsed the wound off with cool river water, applied the herbs, and wrapped her leg with fresh strips. I swallowed the lump twisting in my throat and fought back tears of guilt.

My tummy rumbled, reminding me I'd hardly eaten that day. Between wrangling horses and tending to Moonie, I missed a meal or two. I stood and stretched my aching back. The wraps looked more even and tighter than the previous times. Wet with sweat, I dipped my neckerchief in the basket of remaining river water, swiped it over the back of my neck, and tied it below my chin. It brought some relief.

Spupaleena and Pekam approached, their horses' heads hung low. Sweat tracks ran down the horses' legs and flanks. Pekam's tan chest glimmered in the light from sweat. Spupaleena wiped her brow as she rode in. They smiled at me. The kinda smile that asked if I had finished my chores. The kinda smile that reminded me to remain responsible.

"How is she?" Pekam pointed to Moonie.

I glanced at the one fresh bandage, then the soiled one. "Better. I have one leg left to tend to." I picked up fresh buckskin strips and leaves filled with herbs and pressed them against the next deep cut. *Prove myself.* I fingered the canoe through the buckskin pouch that hung around my neck and reminded myself to keep my opinions in my head.

Spupaleena glanced at her herd of horses, then stared at me stoned-faced for one long moment. I squirmed. Was I doing something wrong? I checked the bandages. I checked the herbs and the ground. Nothing spilled. So I wrapped. But I felt her eyes on me. I hummed to get her out of my thoughts.

They unsaddled their horses and let them loose. A different pair of horses would be worked tomorrow while those two rested. Spupaleena held a rigid rotation schedule: six days on and one day off for each horse. Skumheist met them a short distance away. Close enough to hear their conversation. A conversation I needed to hear.

"I do not think she is taking this seriously." Spupaleena glanced at me.

I frowned. *I'm doing all I can to help Moonie.* My eyes fell to the basket of river water. I took to scrubbing Moonie's leg. I quit humming in hopes of eavesdropping some more. She was determined to send me away. Thoughts of Montana and old Aunt Erma ran wild in my mind. *Please Lord, I need to stay.*

"Give her time," Skumheist said. "She is learning."

Spupaleena frowned. "She should have been done by now. It does not appear as though she has yet taken Moonie down for a drink."

"She has not. But—"

"But nothing, Father. Moonie has not had a drink all day. That same animal that carries her selfish body around and does all that she asks."

"Have you always taken care of your animals the way

you should?" Pekam said. He crossed his arms and shot her a disgusted look.

Spupaleena glared at her brother and turned to her father.

I continued to change Moonie's bandage, pretending I couldn't hear them.

A familiar voice called from afar. "Hellooo!"

My attention bounced between the voice and Spupaleena's next comment.

"She is not ready. This was a bad idea. I should have sent her home." Spupaleena glanced at the woman quickly approaching on a short, stout bay. "She will return home with her mother."

I gasped. *She can't send me home!* With hunched shoulders I peered around Moonie's back end, getting a good look at the woman on the horse. *Mama*! I couldn't decide whether to run to her, or turn and scurry away in the other direction. I slowly rose, feet planted in the dirt. Heavy and unmoving. It was over. My dreams. My chance. All over because of an unexpected downpour. "Blasted storm!"

Spupaleena smiled, waving Mama over to her, and then glancing my way with arched black brows. I dropped my focus to my scuffed boots. I figured she'd wave me over, but didn't. Relief spilled over me like a waterfall on a hot, dusty day. I checked Moonie over a second and third time, brushed her, fed her dried apples, and took her to the river for a drink.

I waded in, taking my sweet time. I heard a little boy laugh and looked over to see Wind Chaser with his little brother, playing with a ball made of buckskin. They were hitting it with sticks, as well as the boy could with a limp. The ball rolled toward me. Wind Chaser glared at me, picked up his brother, and packed him off, leaving the ball behind.

Maybe it's time to leave. No one wanted me there. No one cared. I was in the way—plain and simple.

After Moonie had her fill, I walked her back and put her up. Mama and the other three were still talking. She waved me over. I gulped, trying to move a foot that only wanted to stick to the ground. I thought about waving back, but my hands stuck to my sides as if filled with lead. I let a breath rush out. I threw out the rest of the wash water and turned the basket over to dry.

I can't go home. My focus pulled to one of Pekam's horses in a corral close to Moonie, to Mama, and back to the horse. My thoughts drifted to the conversation with my papa. He agreed to let me stay as long as I obeyed. I reckon I blew it. They will now force me to live with Aunt Erma. As if I had no control, my legs carried me to Pekam's corral. I reached for the rope.

"Stop." Pekam shouted in Sinyekst.

I closed my eyes and dropped my hand to my side.

"It is not worth it." He placed a hand on my shoulder. "Everything will work out."

"But Mama will take me back. I'll be sent to Montana." I faced my uncle.

"My father will talk to her. He will make her see things clearly." He hung onto my wrist and pulled me toward my mama. "I promise."

With heavy steps, I dragged my feet over to Mama and hugged her. She pulled back and gave me a curious look. I gave her a small smile, thinking no one had said anything about me leaving yet. I surely wasn't gonna spill the beans.

Mama untied a parfleche bag from her saddle. "I have cabbage, potatoes, carrots, baked beans, jerked venison, bacon, fixings for biscuits and flapjacks." She untied a second parfleche bag from the other side of her saddle. "If none are broken, I have a few fresh eggs as well." She pulled out two handfuls of scrunched shirts and held them as if they were baby chickens, and looked around. "Should I have brought milk? I don't see your cow."

Pekam laughed. "*Loot*, the cow you gave us years ago is still here. Some of the children in the village have taken her over. And her babies."

"Babies?" Mama arched her blond brows.

"One of the men brought back a young bull from Fort Colvile. It was injured," Pekam said.

Spupaleena chuckled. "They thought it would be dead by the time it crossed the river." She motioned to the river with a thumb.

"He lived. And hooked up with Brown Coat," Skumheist said.

Mama giggled. "Brown Coat?"

"That is what a young girl calls him now," I said with enthusiasm in hopes of keeping the conversation off of me. Everyone had quit laughing but me. I dropped my chin to my chest. Things weren't going as planned. In fact, nothing had been going as planned for a while now.

Everyone turned to me and the conversation died.

I felt my face heat up like a red-hot branding iron. "I'll go finish up." I turned and marched back to Moonie. There was nothing to finish, but they were none the wiser. An urgent rush to flee filled me. *Should I leave now? Wait until tonight when everyone was asleep?*

"What's wrong with your horse, Hannah?" Mama said. "Why are her legs wrapped?"

I jumped at her voice. She was right behind me, craning her neck as she peered around me at Moonie, eggs still clutched as if they were a newborn baby in her arms. Peering over my shoulder, I saw Pekam holding Mama's horse, a frown on his face. He shrugged. I sighed. Do I tell her? Do I let them tell her? Spupaleena held the second parfleche with that notorious hardened look on her face. "I…um…"

Pekam shoved the reins in his father's grasp and strode toward me. When he got to us, he said, "We came off that hill in the middle of a lightning storm," he pointed to the mountain behind them, "I guess Moonie got scared and crashed through the brush."

I stared at Pekam. That's all I could do. My gaze darted to Mama.

Mama examined the soiled bandages. "That tale sounds far-fetched to me. This mare wouldn't flinch at a cougar leaping on her from the top of a fir tree." She handed me the eggs still nestled in Pa's shirts and knelt down for a closer look.

I softly groaned, seeing I'd left the filthy strips on the corral poles. I glanced at Pekam, praying the Lord would drop some kind of distraction from the sky. A loose horse, or better yet a stampede of 'em, or a sudden downpour of rain. Anything.

"Elizabeth, I have no reason to tell you a fib." Pekam knelt down and studied her from the opposite side of the horse's belly. "These are surface scrapes we are putting herbs on and wrapping so there will be no infection."

Mama stood. "I reckon you're telling the truth." She arched her brows in warning.

"Besides, she's already had a go round with having to feed the horses…" His voice trailed off as he realized he'd let more of the truth slip than was planned. His face turned an odd shade of pink.

"I already know about the previous incident. Phillip told me." She turned to me, hands on slim hips. "You are running out of chances. One more and you will never race again. I'll see to it."

I'd never heard Mama speak in such a low, deep growl before. Shivers danced up my arms. "We have another race in a few days. You'll see how good I am. You'll see I can win. You will stay and watch, won't you?"

"Life is not about winning horse races, Hannah," Mama said. "Scratches? Storms? Running off? Doesn't sound like anyone is in control around here. I don't know what you have done to earn such punishment to have to water the entire herd, but it must have been a tremendous act of rebellion."

Pekam placed a hand on Mama's shoulder. "I think—"

She raised a palm to his face. "Don't think, Pekam. I feel lied to. You said nothing would happen. You promised my daughter would obey the rules. Be safe. Don't you see how willful she's become? We keep giving her chances and she only takes them for granted. Enough. Her chances have run out. No more excuses." Mama grabbed the bundle of eggs out of my hands and one spilled out, cracking on the ground. She shook her head, cradled the eggs to her chest, and stomped over to Spupaleena's lodge.

Chapter 10

Mama wiped a tear from her cheek. I hunkered down and hid behind a tree. I had to find out what she was thinking to plan my next move.

"She…she makes my blood boil. That one, stubborn as a wood tick on a deer's belly." Mama paced back and forth in front of the lodge, hands waving in the air.

"Remember now awful I used to be?" Spupaleena said.

"You were never this cantankerous. Not nearly." Mama shook her head, still pacing.

I leaned into the tree. *Cantankerous?* A twig snapped as I stepped back. My heart pounded in my ears. Mama continued to pace and rant, too busy to hear the *crack*. I sucked in a breath and let it out as quietly as I could. Leaned closer to the tree, stepping lightly this time.

"What are you doing?" A high-pitched voice asked in the Sinyekst tongue.

I jumped and shushed a young girl who stood beside me, glancing up. "Go play." I pushed her away.

She hung onto my arm, tugging at me.

"Loot!" She giggled.

"Do not tell me no," I whispered. "Now go. Git. I need to listen."

She giggled, tugging harder.

I again shoved her away. She released her grip and fled. "Good Lord," I whispered, praying they didn't hear the commotion. I again leaned against the tree, pressing in, ear cocked to the ranting. Skumheist had joined them. Two against one. Or that could be in my favor.

"She is trying." Skumheist handed Mama a cup of something. Probably mint tea.

I sniffed the air as if I could smell the aroma. It was her favorite and tended to calm her nerves. I silently thanked Skumheist.

"She will learn her lesson, as my daughter and son did when they were young," Skumheist said. "Is it better she go to Montana and run away or be here with us, learning and growing?"

Mama paced some more. "Do you think she'll ever be a lady?" She turned to Spupaleena and gave her a sheepish look. "I'd rather have her home with me where I can keep an eye on her. Teach her more about herbs. How to be a proper homemaker. With manners." She blew on her tea.

Spupaleena eyed at her father.

He nodded. "I do think she will be a lady. She loves you, Elizabeth. More than anything. She is more like you than she is willing to admit. This will not last. Once she races for a short time, she will settle down and have a family."

"I'm not so convinced." Mama sipped her tea. "She wants to follow your every move, Spupaleena. You have never married. You are independent. Strong." Mama's voice cracked.

"That doesn't mean I will never marry," Spupaleena said.

I choked on her words. My auntie had never talked about marriage before.

"I do plan to marry someday." Spupaleena stepped closer to her friend. "I will talk with her about this. I may even tell her who I have my eyes on." She smiled.

"You are interested in someone?" Skumheist said. "This is the first you have talked about a husband."

"Yes. I know. I am sorry. The horses take up much of my time. I am thinking about not racing anymore, only raising colts. Pekam is ready to take over." Spupaleena glanced in my direction. I darted behind the tree, stepping on the little girl I thought had disappeared.

"*Ayeee*!" She fell on the ground and began to cry.

I scooped her up, holding her close. "I'm sorry. I thought you'd left." She wrapped her little arms around my neck and buried her face in my chest. I comforted her, running my fingers down her hair and back. It felt... motherly.

She sniffed and gazed at me, mumbling in Sinyekst. Her big, brown eyes held downcast assured me she'd recognized her disobedience. Her round, chubby face and doeskin dress with bare feet made me smile instead of scolding her. I held onto her with a firm grip, shushing her. All she'd wanted to do was play. Once her tears dried, I set her down. She scampered away.

"Perhaps there is hope for you after all," Mama said.

I whirled around, smashed my head against the hiding tree, and sprawled out on pine needles and cones. "There is hope. I told you I want to settle down, just not quite yet." I scowled, fingering the bump on my head.

Mama's pursed lips softened. She held out a hand and helped me to my feet. I wiped dirt and leaves from the skirt. She slipped an arm into one of mine, and we strolled over to Spupaleena and Skumheist.

Pekam joined us. "You think we've been dishonest. I know you are upset and if she was my daughter, I would be disappointed as well. Please listen when I tell you she is trying and working hard. She has earned a spot in a race in two days. Some of the boys are beginning to respect her, something my sister took longer to earn. If we let Hannah continue to race, she will see how important it is to listen to us and learn the wisdom we now have trusting our horses and each other." He drew in a breath, eyes wide.

"I see your English has greatly improved." Mama smiled. "I agree, it will help her learn discipline." She fingered the metal tea cup. "But there is something you continue to keep from me."

Pekam nodded. "Spupaleena works with me. I read the books you leave for the children." He peered at me. "You are right. Forgive us for keeping the entire truth from you. Moonie fell when we were coming off the mountain in a storm. It was slick. There was nothing Hannah could do." His face brightened. "As you can see, she is fine."

I gasped, not figuring a twenty-four-year-old man would act like such a schoolboy trying to please his teacher. Mama scanned my body with concerned eyes. I scowled at my uncle for telling her we'd fallen. She didn't need to know. I knew from then on she'd be hovering over me like an anxious hummingbird.

"I'm not foolish. I saw the cut on her forehead. I expect the truth from now on, Pekam." After a long pause, Mama agreed. "I will allow her to ride."

Shocked, I embraced Mama with such force we almost tumbled to the ground. I released her and took a step back. "I will not let you down, Mama. I promise." I cringed, knowing I'd sounded like a schoolgirl.

Mama ran a finger down the side of my face, tucking a stray hair behind my ear. "I remember when you used to sneak off and race with the Spukanee young'uns. You had so much fun. I couldn't believe how well you rode that little pony your pa came home with. I always knew this day would come. And I always knew I wouldn't be able to stop you. But I had to try."

I held Mama's hand. "It's in my blood. It just is. I'm not trying to be cantankerous." I rubbed the pouch around my neck, fingering the canoe. *Slow my mind. Think. Pray.* "I'm simply trying to find my way."

Water pooled in her hazel green eyes as she laughed. "You were listening." Her white and rust-colored gingham dress brought out the green in her eyes. Strands of gray peeked through her blond locks and creases formed in her soft, heart-shaped face. She looked like an angel. My heart ached to please her, but I knew I'd forever regret not racing. Like I told her, it ran deep.

"What's around your neck?"

I slid the wooden canoe out of the pouch around my neck and handed it to her. "Skumheist gave it to me. It's supposed to remind me to stop and think and pray."

Mama fingered the wooden piece. "Is it working?"

"I reckon. A little."

She handed it back to me. "Skumheist is a wise man."

"He is." I placed the canoe back in its protective nest and hung it back around my neck.

Mama grabbed a handful of my skirt. "Looks like we need to make you something more suitable for riding."

I arched my brows. "What do you have in mind?"

"I have an idea. Good thing I brought needle and thread. I planned on mending your pa's shirts while you are all off riding."

"I glanced at her parfleche bag. Is that what the eggs are wrapped in?"

Mama nodded. "They are."

Spupaleena chuckled. "I'll put the eggs in a basket."

I put a hand up to Spupaleena. "I will." I needed to get away and think. This was all too easy. Spupaleena had something up her sleeve. Why didn't Mama ask more about my fall? The fox she is would have every scrap of truth laid out bare before the Lord and me on my knees repentin' and recitin' the Lord's Prayer. It all smelled foul.

Mama nodded. "We'll have to eat them tonight."

"Does that mean flapjacks for supper?" Pekam said.

"Indeed. That does mean flapjacks, ham, and eggs for supper." Mama grabbed my hand. "Come on. We have work to do."

I glanced down. "I have chores to finish." Something snuck past me. A slight glance or nod. I had to find out what they were all planning.

"You help your mother. I will finish the chores." Pekam smiled.

I was now convinced Pekam had been hogtied into the secret plan against me. I'd need to keep my eyes on him. Mama and I spent the rest of the daylight cutting and sewing my skirt, making them look like a wide pair of britches. This new getup would be so much lighter than the buckskin leggings. I grabbed a scrap piece of fabric and sewed a hidden pocket into the inside of my skirt while Mama mended one of Pa's shirts. I tried not to let her see it. I swapped the skirt I had on with the floral, wide-legged riding britches and swirled around.

"A perfect fit!" Mama's eyes danced as she watched me. "Those will work just fine, I'm certain of it."

"Thank you." I hugged her, not letting on I knew something shifty was taking place.

"You always were a spitfire, but I will support your dreams, for now." She winked at me.

Mama to my back, I found my knife and tucked it in the secret pocket of my new riding britches. I patted the metal bulge. *No one will ever know.* Flowers and steel, not many girls paired the two.

"Hannah?"

"Just a minute." I took the knife out, then placed it back in as quickly as I could. Satisfied, I faced her.

"Is something wrong?" She studied the skirt.

"No. Everything is perfect." I smiled, resisting the urge to finger my knife.

Chapter 11

"Tighten your cinch." Mama ran a shaky hand down Moonie's neck.

I scrunched my face. "I will."

"Is the leather strap on your bridle tearing?" Mama leaned in for a closer look.

"It's fine. Pekam already checked everything." I gave her a look that asked her to step back and give me a little space to breathe.

Mama strode over to Spupaleena. "I felt this way when she was little. You'd think my heart wouldn't pound like it does." She fanned her face with her hat.

"She is a strong rider," Spupaleena said. "She will be fine."

"Yes, perhaps…" Mama rubbed the back of her neck.

"Are we ready?" Skumheist planted his feet between his daughter and Mama.

"How do you think she'll do?" Mama turned to Skumheist.

Say something that will distract her. I tightened the cinch then walked Moonie in a few circles.

Wind Chaser strode past. He resembled a cock after

his hens. "Be alert."

I patted the knife in my hidden pocket. "I am. Perhaps you should worry about your horse." His stallion stopped, stretched out, and relieved himself, splashing his waste over Wind Chaser's moccasins.

I smirked. It was all I could do to remain ladylike.

Wind Chaser's face turned several shades of red before he stormed away. He rambled off several Sinyekst works as he walked. I picked up "destroy" and "won't finish." I glanced over at Mama and the others to see if they'd heard anything. There were busy comforting and encouraging her with pats on her back.

"Do not worry about him."

I stiffened at Pekam's comment. "He don't bother me."

"Especially with that knife in your pocket." He spoke in a low tone.

I swirled around and faced him. "You know about my knife?"

"I do not see a bulge, but you keep patting your waist. Do you have one of your father's pistols or a bow in that new riding outfit of yours?" He put his hand out as if to touch the fabric.

I swatted it away. "I do not!" I lowered my voice. "I sewed in a secret pocket. Not even Mama knows about it, so don't you say a word."

A solemn expression on his face, Pekam shook his head and whispered, "I will not say a word to anyone."

I gave him a sinister smile.

"You are brave." Pekam walked past me.

I didn't know if he was making fun of me or was serious. But I took it as a compliment. I contemplated going over and trying to comfort Mama. No, I'd focus on Moonie. I didn't want her worry attached to me. Besides, Spupaleena and Skumheist seemed to be handling her just fine. Three drum beats sounded. I led Moonie to the starting area and swung into the saddle. Hanging back, I circled her around a few times.

A quiet boy I'd known for some time but hadn't paid much attention to rode up beside me. "Keep your eyes in front of you. Do not look back no matter what."

"Why not?"

Two drum beats sounded.

"Running Elk, why not?" Panic surged through me. There was no time to make sure my knife was in its protective spot.

All us racers whirled our antsy horses around and settled them into a crooked line. One thump of the drum sounded and we tore out.

Why can't I look back? I barely turned my head then stopped myself. A boy rammed his horse into Moonie. I shifted to the left, but was able to hang on and drag myself back into the center of the saddle. I pushed my feet down into the stirrups and sank deep into my seat. I glanced over at him and recognized him as the boy who'd given Spupaleena a hard time in the frosted meadows. Hahoolawho's son. Why was he after me? What did I do to him? I pinned my gaze on the rider ahead of me.

The boy rammed into me again. I elbowed him and kicked Moonie. She stuck her nose out, hooves eating up dirt. As we climbed up a hill, the trail narrowed, and the pace slowed. Shadows cast an eerie sensation over the mountains. Odd how the scents of pine and sumac filled my senses at a time like that. But I was glad it did. My muscles relaxed and my head cleared.

With Wind Chaser in the lead and Running Elk a close second, I was in the middle of the pack. I was thankful Running Elk had warned me not to look back. These boys were out for blood. As tight as we were packed in, one wrong move would send us tumbling down the steep slope to my right. A deer jumped down the bank and darted in front of the pack, grazing Wind Chaser's horse. When his horse scrambled to the side, Running Elk gained the lead. Wind Chaser shouted at him, waving a fist in the air as he kicked his horse and darted back onto the trail, crowding me out. We bounded around a curve at the top and dropped down a steep slope. My throat fell into my gut as rocks rolled under the horses' hooves.

Moonie's breaths came deep and fast. I felt the heat off the saddle, my riding-britches whipping in the wind. I made a mental note to hack off the extra width. I leaned back with a hand gripping the cantle of my saddle, trying to stay up-right like the trees on a side hill. One boy with blue paint on his face strained to pass me and without thinking, I slapped him in the face with my reins. He shrieked. I kicked Moonie, keeping my gaze on Running Elk. Blue Face rammed into us. I leaned over and elbowed him in the nose. He backed off after screeching like an infant.

Wind Chaser glanced back, a crazy look on his face. With narrowed eyes, I stared right through him, not letting my quaking body give way to my fear. He turned back around, ramming into Running Elk, who nearly got thrown off. With clenched teeth he pulled himself back on.

The sound of the gingham whipping in the wind made me wonder if the excess fabric slowed us down. My mind on my britches and not what was in front of me, a tree branch slashed my cheek. "Ouch!" I pressed the heel of my hand over the cut. Blue Boy passed me, blood staining his face. I smirked, knowing it had to be from my elbow. No-account deserved it. We jumped over downed trees, probably from the last windstorm, and plunged into a creek. Blue Boy's horse balked. Moonie plowed over the steep bank, leaped into the creek, and lunged forward. While we passed, Blue Boy strained to pull me out of the saddle, but I was able to fight him off and get loose.

Wind Chaser circled to the right and up we went again. The climb was steep. Moonie dug into the rocky terrain and I bounced in the saddle with each step. She puffed, weakening with each step but never losing heart. I gave her the reins and she plowed through her fatigue. Silence drifted behind me. My head jerked back a smidgen before I allowed myself to turn around enough to see the rest of the riders a good clip behind us. *Don't worry about them.* We crowned the top of the hill and slid down the other side. Once the trees opened up and a meadow welcomed us, I reined Moonie to the outside.

Wind Chaser and Running Elk were ahead of me, but not by much.

Aspen leaves and sunflowers waved us on. We surged forward and headed back into the woods. Brush tore my shirtwaist and clawed my arms. A flock of turkeys rose up from the brush, causing our horses to side-step. A yelp from behind us caught my attention. Again I broke the rule, looking back to see Blue Boy's horse shoved over by another rider and slam into a tree. I snickered, realizing it was not ladylike. I felt no remorse. I spun my gaze forward. There was no daylight between the horses and dust that blew up into my face.

I swiped dust from my eyes with my shirt sleeve. It only made things worse. Tears attempted to wash dirt away, but to no avail. I pressed on. The horses were exhausted and beginning to slow down. At this point, I reckoned who craved to win the most would. I prayed it was me.

A crack of daylight poked through swirling dirt. I kicked Moonie, and as we turned a corner, a meadow came into view. We slipped through the crack as though Moonie grew wings. She seemed to draw a fresh batch of get-up-and-go and blew past both Wind Chaser and Running Elk. We stormed past the finish mark, spectators yelling and dancing and clapping. Drums beat a celebratory tune.

By the Lord's grace, I'd won. Now Mama had to let me race.

I circled Moonie into a trot and down to a walk. Pekam trotted over to us, clutching the rein and pulling Moonie to a halt. I hopped down and caught a glance of Mama. Her face shone white as a sheet. My spirits dropped as fast as a stone in water.

"You won!" Pekam lifted me up and twirled me around like he used to when I was small. "How do you feel?"

I turned to him and shrugged. I didn't know how I felt. At first I was happy and in disbelief, but after seeing Mama's expression, I felt sick. Dreading her claim for Montana. I turned to my uncle. "How did it feel when you won that day? When you beat all those men as a young boy?"

"Like fresh salmon after a long winter." Pekam smiled, his eyes shining.

I fingered the canoe. "What was the best part of it?"

Without hesitation, Pekam said, "Listening to Smilkameen laugh. I had not heard that noise come from her lips until that moment. No one had!"

"So I hear." I gazed at Mama. "I better go and see her before she faints."

Mama opened her arms the second I reached her and embraced me with a hug that threatened to squeeze the air out of me. I felt her heartbeat against my chest. Felt her deep sigh. I allowed myself to melt into her embrace. "I'm fine, Mama. I am."

I dropped my arms. "I better tend to Moonie." I wanted to leave before she collected herself enough to change her mind about supporting my dreams. I'd hoped this race would have encouraged her by proving I was an accomplished rider. I feared it did the opposite.

She nodded, wiping tears from her face.

I climbed back into the saddle and turned Moonie toward a creek, intending to soak her legs. Someone grabbed my arm and wrenched me to the ground, pinning me into the dirt. I struggled to breathe. After thrashing for several minutes, I opened my eyes to see Blue Boy's face hovering over mine. The bright red welt from my reins rose from his cheek and blood smeared his face. "What do you want with me?"

Hahoolawho's son knelt beside me and leaned close. "Spupaleena weakened my father. I promised him I would not harm her, but I can get rid of someone she cares about."

"You are nothing but a coward," I said in a low hiss.

I struggled against his grip. "Let me go!"

"My name is Standing Bear. Know I am coming after you! When you are alone, I will be there."

I swear I saw the Devil dancing in his eyes when he spoke his name. "What have I done to you?"

He slapped me. "You try to be one of us." He spat in my face. "Go away. We do not want you here. You are not one of us!"

I jerked as a blur knocked him off me. I managed to stagger to my feet. Running Elk clutched him in a choke hold. I opened my mouth to shout for him to stop then thought better of it. Standing Bear needed a lesson in how to treat women. He wasn't about to stop until I was dead.

Chapter 12

"He won't stop until she's dead!" Mama wrung her hands as she paced in Spupaleena's lodge.

"He won't hurt me." I patted the bulge on my waist.

Mama's gaze dropped to my hand. "What's wrong? Are you hurt? Or ill?"

"No!" I put out a hand as she stepped closer. "I'm fine, Mama. Don't fret, Pekam protects me. He always has."

"He won't be there every time one of these boys tries to knock you off your horse. He wasn't there this time. That other boy knocked him off of you. Who was he? What if they try this nonsense in the woods? No more! I can't..." Tears threatened to pour down Mama's face. She dragged in a deep breath, held it, and let it blow out of her pursed lips.

"Those boys only threaten me. It's only words—"

"He dragged you off Moonie, Hannah. That is more than words. Then the beast spit in your face. I won't allow this." She shook her head until her bun came loose. "I won't!"

Skumheist ducked through the tule-mat flap of the lodge. He nodded at Mama then turned to me. "Go wash in the river. I need to talk to your mother."

Hesitant, I gazed at Mama and slipped out. I found Pekam eating dried salmon in the shade. I debated whether to go wash up or thank him. With Mama dragging me away, I hadn't had a chance to. He waved me over.

"How's that scratch on your arm?" He handed me a buckskin pouch. "This is from Smilkameen." He chuckled. "She walked to the lodge, listened for a minute, shook her head, and stomped off, babbling something about girls not being allowed to ride horses like men."

I eased down beside him and opened the pouch. Pekam handed me a piece of salmon. I shoved it in my mouth, savoring the wild flavor. I dipped a finger in the bag, examined my scratches, and washed the cuts. Medicine wouldn't keep infection from my dirt-and debris-covered body unless the wounds were clean.

"Next time you might want to pull that knife out and use it." Pekam pointed to my waist.

I looked at my waist. "I forgot about it."

He grinned. "I bet you will only forget this one time."

I rolled the salmon around in my mouth, not knowing how to respond, and headed for the river. After gently scrubbing my cuts with sand, I applied salve from the pouch. I sat on the shoreline and stared into the water that reflected soft blue mountains and deep green trees. My mind wandered back to Montana. I could not imagine Mama and Pa sending me there, but with Mama madder than a fox with her tail caught in a trap, I reckoned that was the plan.

Quick, sharp footsteps alerted me to a visitor. My mother's boots. They halted behind me. Shivers ran up my spine and I grew stiff. I waited for her to grab me by the ear and drag me back.

"Come on, we're going home." Mama's voice sounded impatient.

"Home?"

"Yes."

I stood and faced her. "Why?"

"Why? Hannah, really!" She crossed her arms over her chest and tapped her toe.

"I'm not a child anymore. Let me stay and find my womanhood with Spupaleena. She's training me—"

"She's already tried. I don't think you can be broke. Not like one of those wild horses of hers. At least they listen and seem to reason. They respect her enough to obey. You won't budge." Mama shoved her hands on her hips. "You had your chance. You proved this is dangerous, and you can't seem to handle racing or the boys over here."

"I'll come home for a while." I marched past her. "But certain as the sun rises, I'll be back." I mumbled that last bit under my breath.

We made it back to the cabin before sundown. Mama and Pa exploded into one big shoutin' match. I'd never heard them squabble in such a way. Lillian bunched up next to me on my bed and read a book. Or pretended to. She did turn a page or two. After a spell, I couldn't stand the tension any longer, so I rose and paced.

"They gonna send you away?" Lillian's left eye peeked out from a loose strand of reddish-brown hair covering her face.

"Probably gonna try." I pounded one fist in the palm

of the other. "Don't worry, Lilly. I'm not going."

"Whatcha gonna do?" Her voice quivered.

"Not certain yet." I glanced out the window. Dusky shadows spattered the barn and dirt, stopping a runaway attempt at least for tonight. It hadn't worked the last time anyway, as they knew where to find me. I'd have to think past the village. Maybe head south toward Lincoln. Maybe east and live with the Kalispeliwho people for a bit. The more I turned that idea over in my head the more I realized it wouldn't work. I'd stick out like a sore thumb, white flesh and all.

Then it hit me—marriage. The corners of my mouth lifted. Butterflies swarmed my tummy.

The only chance I saw was to hunt down Running Elk. I was certain he'd help me after his rescue. That showed he cares. Perhaps deeply. That way Spupaleena wouldn't find out I'd been to the village. Since there was nothing more I could do, I blew out the lantern. Lillian slept with me. Poor thing shivered from worry and fret. I rubbed her back until she fell asleep. My mind wouldn't turn loose, so I stared at the moon most of the night as it passed over the sky.

Early the following morning, I was about to enter the barn when I overheard Pa and Delbert talking. My brother attempted to persuade our pa to let him escort me to Montana. Jack was busy and it was his duty as the oldest male sibling, he insisted. I snorted. *His duty.* Keen on his part, though. This was my chance. I nodded right along with the eldest boy and his plan.

My brother mentioned a handful of ranchers he'd talked to the previous day while checking on the herd. The men planned to fish a day or two and move on. They were headed to Montana for cattle and said we could team up with them. In my own thoughts, I heard Pa say "all right." I leaned closer to the barn wood, squeezing my eyes shut, not certain I heard them correctly. Footsteps drove me behind the barn. While I sneaked in the back door, Delbert spooked me. I screamed, nearly wettin' my britches.

"How long you been listenin'?" Delbert leaned against the ladder propped against the loft.

"Enough to hear you're taking me to Montana." I grinned.

"Wipe it off your face. We're going to Aunt Erma's."

"What?"

"You heard me."

"I won't go." My gut twisted.

Delbert crossed his legs. "Where did ya think I was takin' you?"

"I can't believe ya sold me out." I stole a glance behind him, hoping no ears were listening. "But I'll go with ya, then stake out on my own."

Delbert laughed. "I figured you'd say that."

I pressed my hands on my hips. "And that's what's gonna happen. You may be the oldest male, I'm the oldest child and you ain't gonna tell me how to live my life."

"Settle down, ya cranky nag." Delbert grabbed a stem of hay and slipped it between his teeth. "I'm not taking you to Montana. Just wanted to see how you'd react."

I smacked my brother's face, hugged him tight, and pushed him away as if he was on fire. "What's your plan then?"

He rubbed the red spot on his cheek. "Nowhere now!"

"I'm sorry. Kind of. You did deserve the wallop for teasing me."

"We head out in the morning and make it look like we're both headed south to hook up with the ranchers. You can double back to the village while I continue on to the Spukanees and bring back some cattle and a horse or two. I'll tell the ranchers Pa changed his mind. I want to research some new ways to grow hay. There are a couple farmers with new ideas near their village. Pa's stuck in the old ways and if I'm gonna take over this place someday, I need to advance ways of doin' things."

"How long you gonna be gone?"

"Don't know. A month maybe."

"You know they'll post a telegram."

"Where from? Lincoln?" Delbert laughed. "That's too far."

I shrugged.

"They trust me. Don't worry." He tossed the hay on the dirt floor. "By the time they realize what's up, they'll know it's for the best." He grunted. "Trying to keep you hog-tied is like trapping a badger. It's a feisty, bloody mess!"

The next morning we rose early, said our good-byes, and rode off. Images of Running Elk galloped across my mind. I shivered, holding back a smile so Delbert's wouldn't catch on. Earlier I'd slipped a pair of his britches on under my skirt for easier riding. He wouldn't need them on his venture with the Spukanees anyhow.

The look on Lillian's face haunted me most of the morning. Her tears supplied me with a heap of guilt that gouged my stomach. The previous day she watched me pack, trying to place one of her dolls in my parfleche so I wouldn't forget her. She acted like I was about to be buried. I knew she'd miss me, but at the same time, she wasn't a little girl anymore and needed to face the hard facts of life—siblings grew up and struck out on their own. She was eleven, for crying out loud. Besides, in a couple days, she'd be over her self-pity and be happy to hog all of Mama's attention.

Like planned and several miles from the cabin, I stripped off my skirt, doubled back, and followed a separate mountain range north toward the village. No way was I going to some old lady I didn't know—relative or not. Ridin' in Delbert's britches was magnificent. I felt light and airy.

By dusk I was close. Not wanting to swim the Columbia River in the dark, I made camp under a pine trees, hobbled my mare, and ate a cold biscuit, hard tack, and dried fruit. Once finished, I washed in the river, crawled in my bedroll, and stared at the stars. My gut agitated like an eddy tossing dirt and debris up against a rock bank. I took out my canoe and turned it over and over.

It was time to figure out a way to hunt down Running Elk without alerting folks to my presence—especially Spupaleena. The more I thought about his rescue, the more I was convinced he was husband material. *Marrying Running Elk would solve all my problems.* I drifted off to sleep, holding my canoe close to my heart, with images of Running Elk strewn across my mind.

Chapter 13

Birds chirped and fluttered from branch to branch, waking me up. Even though I barely saw the opposite side of the river through dawn's dark cover, there was enough moonlight to cross. I imagined Running Elk greeting me on the other side, us holding hands and sharing our plans, then sighed in disappointment knowing he would not be there. With a heavy heart I saddled Moonie, tied my bedroll and boots to my saddle, and mounted. Since no other human was around, I rolled my underclothing up as high as they would go, wrapped the britches around my neck to keep them dry, and shoved my boots and stockings in one of the parfleche bags tied to the saddle.

My bare feet tingled in the frigid water as Moonie waded in. At the drop off she plunged in and soaked my clothing. I shivered in the cold early morning air. Once on dry land, I slipped on dry britches. As I slid on my stockings and boots I glanced upriver, hoping to see Running Elk galloping toward me, long braids bouncing of his muscular chest, a smile on his sweet face. I sighed, seeing no one, mounted my mare, and headed for the Sinyekst village.

The sun angled high and hot by the time I reached

the south edge of the village. On a bluff overlooking the river perched Spupaleena. I searched for trees to hide behind, but there were none. I was opened and exposed. Eyes narrowed, she shot me a searing look, as if she'd known I was coming. My thoughts rambled with excuses and reasons for being there—none of them decent.

"What are you doing here?" she asked.

"I've come to train." I clutched my pouch, running a finger over the side of the canoe.

Spupaleena frowned. "What about Montana and *Wussa* Erma?"

"You of all people should know I never intended to go." I glanced past her and rested my gaze on the mountains.

"I will not hide you, *Kook Yuma Mahooya*."

I stiffened as she called me by my Sinyekst name. "I didn't come here for you." Not waiting for a reply, I went in search of Falling Rain. I hoped she was still with her father and not in the mountains with the huckleberry pickers.

I found her sitting by a morning cooking fire, her eyes hollow and tired-looking. I rode up, dismounted, and ground-tied Moonie. Big-eyed, she set her cup aside and stood, glancing at her father's lodge. "I cannot be with you."

"Not at all?"

"My father says you are bad medicine and harm is coming your way." She hugged me. "I am sorry. You must leave."

Falling Rain's face looked as pale as it had weeks ago. Tears threatening to fall, I turned and hurried into the woods, not wanting to cause her further distress. I stopped at a creek and plopped down on a bed of grass. Hot tears streamed down my cheeks. I hugged my knees. *Why, Lord?*

My gaze lifted to the horizon and in my view stood Running Elk. I sprang to my feet. "What are you doing here?" My hand flew to my heart.

"I saw you rush off…so I followed." He took a few steps forward. "I thought you were gone."

I shook my head. "I refuse to go. I can't leave…" I took a step toward him, desperately needing to tell Running Elk how he could help me, but the words stuck in my throat.

He took another step forward.

With great restraint I threw my hands out in front of me. His closeness both thrilled and frightened me.

He took hold of them. "Does Spupaleena know you're here?"

"Yes," I whispered, shifting my gaze to the creek.

"Hannah." His voice, soft and enticing, pulled me toward him.

How could I be so happy and scared at the same time? Was this really happening? So quickly? I couldn't look at him. His coal-colored eyes made me tremble. My mind told me to run, but my legs wouldn't budge.

"Come with me. Let's go somewhere—"

His touch weakened my knees.

"Run away with me." His warm hands cupped the sides of my face.

I turned to him. "Falling Rain can come so no one talks…" I paused. My heart screamed yes. Commonsense told me to run home. "I don't know…" I wrung my hands.

"Think about it. Meet me back here before the sun sets." He turned and trotted off.

He disappeared through the trees. I chastised myself for letting him go. Of course I wanted to run away with my future husband. This was my path to freedom. Boots off and trousers rolled up, I strolled up the creek and let the icy water numb my body. Conflicting thoughts rushed me like a pounding waterfall. Go with him! And do what? Live where? Would Falling Rain come with us? Could I talk her into it? I grunted.

After some time, I trekked back to the village and spotted Falling Rain with her father. I walked by, trying to catch her attention with a slight wave. She held her gaze on the garment she mended. Her father stared at me, a scowl on his face.

I waited in the shade at the far end of the village, teaching small children English words. They giggled at one another as they practiced new words. I kept one eye on the children and the other on Falling Rain's father, hoping he'd leave so I could try and convince Falling Rain to come with us.

It was a long time before Falling Rain grabbed two deer bladders and headed toward the river. I shooed the children away and followed her. There was no sign of her father, which made me breathe easier, but I was still on the lookout.

"Why are you following me?" Falling Rain dropped the bladders. "I will be punished."

"Running Elk and I met. We want to run away—"

"Leave me alone!"

"Listen. Please."

Falling Rain stiffened.

"I want to be with Running Elk, but we can't be alone."

Falling Rain peered at me, mouth open.

"Come with us." I picked up one of her bladders and dipped it in the creek. "I know you are unhappy here. I see it in your eyes." I desperately wanted to tell her the truth. How Running Elk would free me from my folk's confinement. I knew she needed the same freedom. She'd probably think I'd gone mad.

Falling Rain looked down. "He will beat me."

I handed her the full bladder and grasped the other one. "That's why you must come with us." I dipped it in the water.

"I cannot," Falling Rain whispered.

"Please, come with us." I handed her the other bladder. "Wait for my signal."

Falling Rain shook her head and rushed back to the village. I prayed she'd change her mind. I hiked up the hill to Spupaleena's lodge. It was empty. I unsaddled Moonie, placed her in an empty corral, and nibbled on a dried apple.

I spent the rest of the day making arrows and a bow from yew wood, thankful Skumheist had taught me a few years back. When finished, I ran my hand down the wood, picking up a couple splinters. I then rummaged outside Pekam's lodge for feathers. Finding none, I searched under trees down the meadow and found enough for five arrows, wrapped them in buckskin and slipped them in my parfleche bag.

A relentless nudge urged me to find Falling Rain to see if she had changed her mind. I spotted her in the shade with other young women making baskets. I caught her gaze and gave her a slight wave with my bow. With an expressionless face, her eyes skimmed over it as she continued to weave. I kept walking.

Still too early to meet Running Elk, I went for a ride, and scanned the lowlands for huckleberries. Not finding any, I searched for other berries. After a while I came across a few tall bushes of serviceberries and picked from Moonie's back.

The faint sound of crunching leaves and broken twigs resounded behind me. Bits of horse and human peeked through trees until Spupaleena and Pekam came into full view. I prayed they'd keep riding, but they saw me and rode over.

"I'll leave in the morning." My half-truth stuck in my throat.

Pekam tipped his head toward the village. "My belly groans. Time to eat."

We turned our horses toward their lodges. I tried to act normal, knowing not much snuck past those two. No words were exchanged between us. Part of me felt horrible and awkward. The independent part knew I'd made the right decision.

As dusk crept in, Spupaleena and Pekam went to visit their father. I slipped away and saddled Moonie as quickly and quietly as I could. I crept to the tree line then rushed to the creek. Running Elk was already there, sitting on his horse. A grin flashed over his face and he waved. Heart pounding, I waved back.

"Where is Falling Rain?" I glanced behind him.

"I hope she will come."

"Me, too." I nodded. "Let's wait. Her eyes looked hopeful when I saw her earlier."

Running Elk pointed to my bow. "You have been

busy."

I grinned. "I have. Reckon we need to eat."

He tossed me a buckskin quiver with a string tied around it. "You may need these."

"How did you know?"

He chuckled. "I saw you making it."

"When?"

He pointed behind me.

Falling Rain's outline loped toward us.

I bowed my head and thanked the Lord. "She came."

Worry covered her face. Body trembling, she reined her horse to a stop.

"You made the right decision," I said.

She shrugged. "I hope so."

"I knew she would listen to me." Running Elk smirked.

I held out my quiver. "We have weapons."

Falling Rain retrieved a bone knife out of her moccasin legging and held it up. "Two bows, arrows, and a knife, we should survive." Her mood seemed to lighten.

Running Elk motioned to the hills with his jaw. "We need to go. It will be dark soon."

I examined all directions as we headed northwest, making certain no one followed. The glow of the moon shed enough light to pick our way up the mountain. At one point the path leveled out and I thought we might stop, but Running Elk kept going. We finally stopped when the moon hung high over our heads. Falling Rain and I laid our bedrolls in the grass, tossing cones and twigs to the side. Running Elk laid his out close enough to see us, but far enough to give us privacy.

"I will keep cougars from sniffing around you,"

Running Elk said from under his blanket.

Falling Rain and I giggled. We lay under the covering of twinkling stars. It led me to mull over life with Running Elk. Perhaps we would travel, gathering a large herd of horses. Raising a passel of young'uns. I knew life would be rugged at times, but I was up for the challenge. What could go wrong with Running Elk by my side?

Chapter 14

My eyes cracked open as the sun skimmed the earth. I glanced toward Running Elk, ready to start our new life. He was gone! I leaped to my feet and rushed over to where he'd slept, tracking his footprints. They lead toward the side of the mountain. I followed for a while, convinced he'd lost his nerve.

"Running Elk ran back to his mama." I tied my bedroll onto the back of my saddle.

Falling Rain grunted, fished in her buckskin pouch, and pulled out two cakes of bannock, handing me one. "I love these cakes. They are worth trading dried salmon for flour with the Hudson Bay men."

I arched a brow at her.

"He is not a runaway. Nor a coward. I think he is hunting." Obviously over her fear of leaving the village, she sank her teeth into the flat bread.

"I hope you're right." I took a bite, wishing I had huckleberries to go with it. I imagined juice squirting into my mouth, its tartness dripping down my throat. It remained dry as dust. I spit it out.

Falling Rain sat on the ground and leaned against her saddle. "He will be back. Come, there are huckleberries in this area."

I followed, dragging my feet. "How long should we wait?" I rummaged through my pack, found dried apples, and handed some to Falling Rain.

"Until he comes."

I groaned. "How long will that be?"

"Waiting is hard for you."

I nodded, hand pressed against my belly. "I reckon it is."

We found a few bushes of huckleberries and picked, keeping one eye out for bears. We had filled two small pouches when Running Elk showed up. I sprang to my feet, rage roaring.

"I have a couple rabbits to go with those." He pointed at the berries with the carcasses.

"Where were you? Why didn't you wake us and tell us where you were going?" I said.

"You both looked peaceful. I was not about to wake either of you." He slid off his horse and wrapped his arms around me. "I will not leave you. Ever."

We trekked back to camp, roasted the rabbit over a low fire, ate part of it, and saved the rest for the next meal.

Bellies full, we packed our belongings and headed up hill. The climb was treacherous. We rested our horses several times until we reached the top. Trees covered miles of mountains while wildflowers of all colors painted the nooks and crannies. The air felt cool and crisp. A slight breeze whispered to us as though it was Koolenchooten's breath.

"I could live up here." I gave Running Elk a sideways glance, probing his reaction.

"Not with snow as tall as Moonie's belly." He

scowled.

I cocked my head. "Reckon not."

"We need to keep going." Running Elk kicked his horse.

The climb down the other side was just as steep. I tried to sit upright, straight as a tree, as we wound our way down. My back ached by the time we leveled out. By the look on her face, Falling Rain felt the same, even though she never complained.

After some time, we made it to a hidden meadow surrounded by mountains and trees. A stream ran along the edge and down the length of the grassy flatland. Birds sang joyous songs all around us. Squirrels and chipmunks quarreled, scampering around trees. The aroma of grass, brush, and wildflowers wafted through the air. I plucked a leaf from an unknown bush and rubbed my fingers on each side. Then rubbed the scent under my nose. An uncontrollable craving for more came over me. I continued to smell the deep green leaf and my fingers. I opened the pouch around my neck and placed the leaf next to my canoe.

"I will go set snares. Then fish when I return." Running Elk turned his horse and rode away.

"He's always so direct," I said. Yet his mysterious ways wheedled me like a worm on the end of a hook.

"His snares will keep our bellies full." Falling Rain slid off her mare, unsaddled, and hobbled her horse in the thick patch of grass near the creek.

"What should we do?" I unsaddled Moonie and hobbled her close to the other mare.

"Father does not allow women to fish." Eyes shining, she broke out into a wide grin. "He is not here to stop me."

"Do you have a pole?" I asked.

"A pole?" she laughed. "We will build a rock weir and let them come to us."

We spent most of the day building the weir that arched from one edge of the creek to the other in a shallow spot south of camp. We found as many head-sized rocks as we could and lugged them to the creek, lining them from bank to bank. The water pooled behind the wall. We filled cracks with smaller rocks.

"Are we catching them with our bare hands?" I looked at my palms, the water, and Falling Rain.

"*Loot.* There are three nets in my pack."

"Good. Never have been able to catch fish with my hands."

Falling Rain fetched the nets and handed me one. "You have tried?"

"Yep. Me and Delbert. Didn't catch one in a pool of thirty or so." I fingered the netting. "What is this made from?"

"The insides of tule stalks."

My tummy growled. "What do we have left for food?"

"I have bannock, one piece of dried salmon, and some of the hackberries we picked last night." Falling Rain groaned. "I meant to bring black camas..."

I dug through my bag. "I have dried fruit, biscuits, and hardtack." I tried to sound hopeful, but wasn't. My mouth watered for Ma's beef stew, fried cabbage, and beans. I was sick of dried food. I opened my mouth to complain, but didn't wanna hurt Falling Rain's feelings. Like her, I kept my grumbling to myself.

Falling Rain studied the mountains. "Tamarack sap is

good. Once hardened it tastes sweet."

"Ma taught me to recognize which mushrooms we can eat and which are poisonous."

"*Loot.* It is the wrong time of year." Falling Rain pushed to her feet. "I am certain we can find something out there."

We grabbed a couple pouches and set out for fresh food. Once in the woods, we hunted for anything edible. By then my tummy felt like an abandoned bee hive.

Falling Rain pointed to a grove of Lodgepole pine. "See the black moss?"

"Yeah." I cringed. "What do you do with it?"

"We steam it for two moons, then eat it. But…"

"What?"

"It can be eaten right off the tree branch. Our hunters do when gone for several days." Her voice grew sorrowful. "We eat it off the branch when there is not enough food."

I fingered the canoe through my pouch. "I reckon it might taste…" I couldn't think of the right word. Nor what it felt like to be that hungry. Back home we had plenty. And with Ma's root cellar, our food kept cool and fresh.

Falling Rain knelt on the back of her horse, broke off a branch, and hooked a string of the black, coarse moss. "Try it."

I plucked off a small piece and set it on my tongue, tried to smile, and spit it out when Falling Rain looked away. Ugh. Bitter. I'd never survive on that.

We continued our search. But because we were in the low country, we came up empty. By the time we got back to camp, Running Elk had returned. He tossed me a handful of horsetail stems. "Smooth your bow with those."

His expression held stern and that concerned me. "How was your hunt?"

He hesitated. "I placed a few snares around and found some willow for the nets." He squinted, glancing behind him.

Falling Rain and I exchanged worried looks. He took one of the three pouches from around his neck. "Thought you might like these." He slid off his horse and handed it to me, slowly swinging me around so my back was in the direction he'd come from while we both clutched the neck strap.

I set the horsetail stems on the grass and opened the pouch, pouring huckleberries into my palm. "What did you get Falling Rain?" I gave her teasing grin and shoved them into my mouth.

He lifted a second pouch from around his neck and tossed it to her. "More." He grinned, scanning the woods behind me as if protecting us from a predator.

"And for you?" I playfully grinned back.

He held up a third pouch. "These are mine." He seemed to relax, his focus now on me.

We ate left-over roasted rabbit and huckleberries with our feet in the creek. The rabbit meat filled our empty bellies, but would have tasted better had it been heated. Life turned from looming to hopeful in a matter of moments all due to a handful of tart, purple berries and the thoughtfulness of one handsome, but distracted fella.

Running Elk motioned to the weir with his head. "You two have been busy."

"We have." Falling Rain pointed downstream. "We found most of the rocks over there. Now we wait."

"You make it sound easy," I said.

"It is." Running Elk stood. He turned to Falling Rain. "Is there an extra net?"

She pointed to her saddle. "In the pack."

Running Elk retrieved the net and three two-foot long willow sticks. He and Falling Rain fastened the nets on the supple limbs and tied them on with strings of tule fiber. The three of us tip-toed into the creek, searching for sign of wiggling fish. I saw a trout, plunged my net in with a scooping motion, and missed. My fish swam away. The other two laughed, Falling Rain covering her mouth.

Running Elk hunched over. "Use quiet, slow movements. Take your time."

I sighed. *Patience.* I fingered my canoe. Running Elk deftly scooped a trout into his net. He smiled at me. With soft steps, Falling Rain moved farther into the pool and dipped her net. She too scooped up a fish. With a nod, she encouraged me to try again.

With slow movements, I dipped my net in and followed a trout. The darned fish wiggled away. "I can't…"

Falling Rain pointed to my net and nodded.

It took all I had to stop myself from slapping the water. I breathed in deeply and focused on the wiggling fish. I tried again, eyeing a big one. With all the patience I could muster, I eased my net into the pooled creek water and scooped up a fish. "I got one!" Fish scattered and swam away.

Falling Rain cheered. "Come clean the fish."

I cringed at the slimy creatures. Pa always cleaned my

fish, knowing I had a weak stomach. I glanced at Falling Rain, brows arched.

Running Elk laughed. "I will go check my snares."

I swallowed my repulsion, and after the fish were cleaned, I started a fire and roasted our catches on sticks over low flames, saving one for Running Elk. When only the bones were left, I wiped my oily fingers on my britches and stood to get more. I was hooked!

Later that evening, Running Elk came back.

"Get anything?" I asked.

Red-faced he said, "*Loot.*"

"Nothing?" Normally a successful hunter, I thought he was teasing.

"We have fish, bannock, berries, and dried fruit." Falling Rain held up several sticks of roasted fish. "This should fill our bellies. I am certain in the morning a critter will be in your snares."

Doubt slithered in, crowding out my hope.

Chapter 15

The next morning we finished off our food. I had no idea it would be this hard to find fresh meat. I was used to Mama's garden and our fresh beef. Good Lord, I missed her cookin'. If we were hungry, we'd walk out the cabin door and dig up something out of the dirt. Fresh and dried meat was stored in the cellar. We had fresh milk. Homemade bread and cakes. What had I given up? I glanced at Running Elk. *Is he worth it?*

Running Elk patted his wash-boarded belly, which made me tingle inside. "Come, run a race with me."

"On foot?" Falling Rain said.

I stifled a snicker. "I think he means on horses."

"But—"

"But nothing. Your Pa's not here to say no." I plopped my hands on my hips, realizing I acted just like my mama. I cringed.

She shrugged her shoulders.

"He'll never find out." I grabbed her wrist and led her to her hobbled mare.

I saddled Moonie. The other two rode bareback.

"Wait," he said.

I glanced at Falling Rain. She shrugged.

He came beside me and uncinched my saddle. "Ride bareback."

"Bareback?" I cinched it back up. "I don't have your balance. You are used to riding without a saddle." I shook my head.

Falling Rain picked up her wooden saddle. "I will ride with mine if that makes you feel better." It was an odd structure made from cottonwood and rawhide with tall horns at both ends. A blanket rested between the horse's back and the saddle with a folded blanket between the saddle and rider's hind end.

"*Loot*!" Running Elk once again uncinched my saddle. He sneered at Falling Rain and motioned for her to set hers on the ground. With a scowl she complied.

I groaned, slid the saddle off Moonie, and set in on the grass. With an extra-hard *whack*, I settled the pad on top.

Falling Rain set hers back down.

They hopped on their horses with ease. I tried to lift myself up with a couple hops, but failed. I led Moonie over to an old log and heaved myself on her back. The other two looked at me like I was about to give them something bitter to taste.

"Well? Let's go!" The word patience came to mind. I scoffed and planted the pouch hung around my neck inside Delbert's shirt. As heavy as Falling Rain's doeskin dress and leggings were, I was amazed by her agility. I was thankful for boys' britches. I couldn't imagine hopping up on Moonie with a dress and all the underclothing required by a lady. But then again I'm no lady. Not yet anyway.

We raced up and down the meadow and somehow I managed to stay on. Until Running Elk had another harebrained idea.

"We could attach leaves on sticks and shoot them with arrows." He turned and rode into the woods. A loud war-whoop echoed through the valley.

"This will be fun!" Falling Rain said.

I rolled my eyes, nearly toppling off Moonie. I swear I saw my horse roll her eyes, too. "I do not favor a bow like you two. I'll watch from over there." I turned to ride off.

"*Loot!*" Her sharp voice sliced the air.

I spun Moonie around and faced her, eyes wide. "Why not?" I'd never heard her use such a tone.

"I will teach you. It is easy."

"Easier than fishing with a net?"

Falling Rain laughed. "Much easier."

I doubted that, but agreed to give it a try. Falling Rain and I rode to the opposite side of the meadow. She insisted we remain seated on our horses since we'd be riding them and shooting from that height. I groaned. But knew she was right.

She pinned a leaf to a tree with sap, moved back beside me on her mare, and drew an arrow. After drawing back her bow, she released. A *swoosh* stung the air. The *thwack* the arrow made into the tree echoed. She made it look so easy.

An over-exaggerated sigh escaped my lips. "Give me a rifle and I can kill a spider on a rock at twenty yards. I am not certain I can hit a leaf with a stick."

Falling Rain chuckled. "Pretend it is your last meal."

I pulled one arrow out of my quiver and fit it to my bow. "Ouch!" Another splinter broke skin. I scolded myself for not smoothing the wood earlier with the horsetail stem then tried to line myself up with the leaf.

Not sitting square, I bumped Moonie with my knees, asking her to circle a couple steps to the right. She did.

With a held breath, I pulled the string back, and aimed. *My last meal. But it isn't your last meal*, my mind told me. I sat on my horse and quarreled with myself until Falling Rain cleared her throat and told me to release. I shook my head, flinging the thoughts out, and released. I was surprised to see the arrow stick in the tree a hair below the leaf.

"*Host*!" Falling Rain nodded and smiled.

"That was a fine shot!" I exhaled. "But it didn't hit the leaf."

"You were close." Falling Rain motioned to the quiver slung over my back. "Try again. This time pull your arrow back farther."

I slid out a second arrow, rubbed my canoe, and tried again. This time I pulled my arrow back as instructed and my arms stopped quivering. One eye closed, I aimed at the leaf and released. This time the arrow stuck in the tree toward the top edge of the leaf.

Falling Rain rode to the tree and pulled my arrows.

I took my arrows from her and stuffed them into my quiver. "I missed."

"Keep practicing. I will go help Running Elk." Falling Rain whirled her mare around and trotted off.

The quick, sharp hoof beats pounded her words into my mind: *host, host, host.* "Yes they are fine shots, but I need to keep practicing. They are not good enough." I stared at the leaf and pictured a spider in the middle of it. I imagined him taunting me. Heard him laugh at me, said I was a sore shot. "I'm gonna roast you for supper." With a dry mouth, I took a third arrow out of my quiver and fit it to my bow. I pulled back, took aim, and released. I smiled at the sound of the *thwack*. Lifted my chin.

I rode to the tree and tapped the end of my arrow with my bow. I'd finally hit the leaf. I turned to the others to share my triumph, but they were busy sticking leaves to the top of three-foot sticks for the course. Running Elk seemed distracted as he worked, continually scanning the woods. I didn't know what seemed to spook him. I shot the rest of my arrows and pulled them out of the tree. The tattered leaf floated to the ground. I slid off Moonie and picked it up. The holes provided proof. I slid it into my britches and found a rock big enough to heave myself onto Moonie's back.

I loped over to the other two, studying the course. "Is it ready?" Six sticks with leaves pasted to the tips crisscrossed down the meadow.

"*Naux new*," Running Elk said.

One more. He pasted the back of the last leaf with sap and stuck it on a thick stick that was already buried deep in soft dirt. Turning to me he asked, "How did you do?"

I pulled out my leaf and handed it to him. "Now are you finished?"

"Much better!" Running Elk handed the leaf to Falling Rain and hopped onto his horse, bow and quiver slung over his back. "Ready?"

"Much better!" She handed me the leaf.

A broad smile on my face, I patted Moonie. "I'll go saddle up."

"*Loot*! You can ride with no saddle." Running Elk scowled. "I will go first." He loped his horse to the start of the stick course.

With a groan, I remained bareback.

Reluctantly I followed, studying the course intently. Running Elk stopped north of the first target, held his bow and arrow out in front of his chest, and nodded to us.

We glanced at each other. Falling Rain's face shone with confidence. My insides twisted with anxiety.

He kicked his horse into a lope and aimed. He let his first arrow loose and kept going. Within seconds he'd shot all six arrows and turned back toward us. He made this look easy. Too easy. My stomach twisted like fists wringing water out of soaked tea towels as he loped toward me.

"I will go next." Falling Rain readied her bow and first arrow. Her arrows had orange rings painted in the center.

Not noticing before, I pulled one of mine out from the quiver. Yellow ringed the middle. My mind drifted to the previous evening. Falling Rain and I talked by the creek while Running Elk snuck off by himself. He must have painted the rings, having planned this little race all along.

With an exaggerated smile Running Elk rode beside me and halted. I gave him a small smile. One I thought gave my apprehension away.

"Did you paint our arrows?" I held one out.

He chortled and turned his attention to Falling Rain.

Falling Rain nodded and kicked her horse into a lope. She drew back and shot her first arrow, then the second, third, fourth, fifth, and sixth. I glanced at the grass, not seeing any arrows stuck in the ground. The ride was smooth. Effortless. How could she have shot so well when her father had not allowed her to ever participate in such manly games? She had been fooling me all along!

With trembling fingers, I tugged my bow off my back and slid an arrow out of the quiver. I gave Falling Rain an anxious grin and kicked Moonie into a walk. My nervousness caused me to wobble.

I pinned my sights on the first stick near the ground, thankful it was near the grass. Orange and blue striped arrows stuck in the stick. I suspected this would be the case for the rest of them. I pulled back, aimed, and released. The arrow hit the grass with a soft whisper. My mouth went dry and my hands were slippery with sweat.

Still at a walk, I mopped my brow with my shirtsleeve and drew a second arrow. Still staring forward, I focused on the second stick. Once again I drew back. This time I willed an image of a spider into my thoughts. Pretended my hands gripped a rifle. Aimed. Held my breath and released. To my surprise, the arrow hit the stick near the grass. Dirt sprayed. I gasped and sat taller, chin up.

I kicked Moonie into a slow trot, tugged a third arrow out of the quiver, and fit it to my bow. I drew back as far as I could, aimed, and released. One of Moonie's steps jerked my body and arrow to the right. I didn't have time to see where it landed as I was busy pulling my mare back to a walk. I felt like cursing, but held my tongue. I was not about to glance back.

I tugged another arrow out and managed to finish the blasted course at a walk. Once I shot the last arrow, I halted and slid off Moonie.

Chapter 16

We'd spent four days fishing, riding, and honing shooting skills from several different courses. Today was no different. Our skills improved every day but this one. At least for me. I couldn't seem to hit a target inches away. I pulled four arrows out of the grass, one from a target, and the other I was still looking for when the other two came and helped me search. I was uncertain if they felt sorry for me, or hated to lose arrows. After some time, Falling Rain found it stuck in the dirt a few horse lengths away.

"What now?" I prayed we were done shooting bows and arrows for now. Even though my arms grew stronger, they were tired.

"I want to race." Falling Rain looked half scared with big eyes and hunched shoulders.

I caught Running Elk's gaze. "We have been for the past five days."

"I mean when we return."

Frankly, the past several days had been blissful. I enjoyed our time together, especially with Running Elk. In fact, I liked the idea of him as my husband more each day. He was kind, attractive, and helpful. I became quite fond of him. And I was used to us three and our freedom.

Running Elk nodded. "We will leave tomorrow. I will set up a course and we can practice, pretending it is a real race."

"Leave tomorrow? Why? I like it here," I said.

"You thought we would live here?" Falling Rain shifted her focus to Running Elk.

"She is right. We have to go back. Our families will be worried."

I looked from Falling Rain to Running Elk, opened my mouth to protest, and changed my mind. How could I tell Running Elk he's the answer to my problem and make it sound reasonable? We needed more time together. More time for him to have affections for me.

Running Elk proceeded to lay out a course: up a hill, curve around and down, through the creek, over a series of logs, in and out of the targets, and back to camp. "The first one off and standing in the creek wins."

"Stand in the creek?" I point to my boots. "I have laces. You two can slip off your moccasins and be in the water a lot sooner than I can." I held up a hand. "Leave?"

"Then you better ride fast." Running Elk laughed. "Yes. We have to go back."

"You could ride barefoot," Falling Rain said. "We all can."

Still stewing about leaving, I kicked my boots to the ground and peeled off my stockings. The other two flung their moccasins to the side. I would ride their silly race, and then worry about convincing them to remain longer.

We mounted and made our way to a log Running Elk dragged over as a starting line. We lined up in front of the log.

"We go on my call." Running Elk glanced at us.

I grabbed a hunk of mane and wrapped my legs around Moonie's sides. "I'm ready."

Running Elk let loose a shrilling cry. Moonie shot forward with the other horses. Because she stayed straight, it was easy to keep my balance.

We followed the course, Running Elk in the lead. The farther we rode, the more comfortable I felt and at one point, I thought I'd beaten him. Until we began to weave in and out of the stick targets.

After the second target I lost my balance and plummeted to the ground, hitting my head on a rock. The force shot me forward, rolling at an uncontrollable speed. My faced flopped in dirt and grass. Dirt shoved up my nose and I had to blow it out. Moonie dashed away with the other horses. Slowly, I pushed myself up, staggered to the creek, and washed my face.

Falling Rain rushed over to me. "Are you hurt?"

I hugged my ribs. "A little sore."

She placed an arm around me for support. Running Elk joined us, Moonie in tow, and helped lay me down in the frigid water—clothes and all. I soaked in the creek until my entire body went numb from the neck down. The other two were busy building a fire, tending to horses, and making me a soft bed. I crawled over and lay down. "Have any willow bark?"

"I will get you some." Falling Rain grabbed a pouch and jogged away.

I liked the thought of being alone with Running Elk, pain and all.

"You scared me." He sat beside me and held my hand.

His touch comforted me. I glanced at him, holding my stomach with my free arm. "I scared myself."

"From now on ride with your saddle."

"No!" I clenched my teeth. "I can learn to ride with no saddle."

"I want you safe."

"I'll be safe."

He leaned over and kissed my hand.

I studied his concerned face. "Train me to race bareback. I promise I'll be safe. This is just a bruise. I won't race until I'm ready…please…"

He lay down next to me, reclaiming my hand. "I can't…I care about you too much to see you injured."

"I care about you, too." I prayed Falling Rain would take her time.

"You are all I think about. I…"

"I'll be fine. I have to because I want to be with you forever. Be your wife." The words spewed out all on their own. I'm sure that was another unladylike behavior, but I could not help myself. He had to know how I felt.

He grinned. "I want you to be my wife."

"I dream we ride and talk and laugh together all day long."

He kissed my hand again. His lips were warm and gentle on my skin. "I think when we return we should—"

"Here, chew on this." Falling Rain's tone was as sharp as the edge of Pekam's knife. She shoved a branch of willow bark in my hand and pinned a warning look on Running Elk. "Go gather wood."

Running Elk stomped away.

I peeled the bark from the willow and shoved a small slice in my mouth. *We should what?* Why did Falling Rain have to interrupt? Did she not see we were talking? She could have waited a little longer. I draped my arm over my face.

Falling Rain placed hot rocks in an old, dented tin can of water and added willow bark. Once it boiled, she handed me the tin cup.

"We were talking." I glared at Falling Rain.

"Looked like more than talking."

I fingered the cup. "Nothing happened."

She grunted then pressed my ribs, a little too hard.

I sucked in a sharp breath.

"They are not broken." She grabbed her net and headed for the creek.

I closed my eyes, taking in slow, shallow breaths. *What was he about to say?*

A crackling fire roused me from a long slumber. Falling Rain and Running Elk sat by the fire, roasting fish. I pressed a hand to my ribs and lumbered over to the fire, settling myself in between them. The sun dangled just above the mountains. Spicy scents wafted by allowing me to relax enough to enjoy the chirps of crickets.

After we ate—in silence—and I'd drank enough willow bark tea to ease my pain, I lay back down on my bedroll. The other two came over.

"I am sorry for interrupting you two. I know nothing would have happened," Falling Rain said.

"It's okay. I'm sorry too." I guessed they must have talked while I slept and sorted things out, which made me glad because I hated harsh feelings to come between the three of us, especially due to a misunderstanding.

Running Elk stretched out on one side of me,

holding my hand, and Falling Rain lay on the other side.

"Tell us one of your grandfather's stories, Running Elk." Falling Rain clasped her hands behind her head.

He stared at the sky for a moment. "Before I tell the story, you must know I believe someone is stealing game from my snares. There are footprints at every trap and they are not ours."

"Is that why you keep watching the trees?" I said. "Should we track him?"

Running Elk shook his head. "Not now. It will be dark soon."

"Who do you think it is?" Falling Rain sat up and studied the woods.

"I do not know."

"Then tell us that story so we get our minds off the intruder." I squeezed his hand.

Falling Rain lay back down, scooting next to me. I groaned as she bumped my ribs.

"Grandfather tells many stories and for some reason, this one sticks in my mind. Northern Lights had five sons: Cold, Colder, Coldest, Extreme Cold, and Most Extreme Cold."

"Mmm." Falling Rain nodded. "I like this one."

"The youngest son acted as scout, freezing leaves and grass. He returned to his father and reported that he'd gone as far as he could. The eldest son would then finish the work. The other three sons stayed up north with their folks."

"Was Northern Lights their Ma or Pa?" I asked.

"Mother." Falling Rain said.

"What was his Pa's name? Aurora Borealis?" I smiled, hoping they'd see the humor.

"What is Aurora Borealis?" Running Elk asked.

"It's another name for Northern Lights." With gritted teeth I slowly wiggled, trying to find a more comfortable position. "Trappers from the northern territory tell stories of the lights that fill the sky with dancing colors at the Hudson Bay camp."

"I have heard of the dancing lights." Running Elk nodded. "The family lived in an ice lodge and could not endure heat of any kind. They jealous of Extreme Cold and guarded him well, not wanting him to get sick from the heat. But he became restless and traveled south. Before he left, Northern Lights warned him not to speak to any humans because he would kill every one he met with his frigid temperature."

"Did they not care? Why send a child into danger?" I wondered if my folks thought I was catapulting myself into danger, when I saw it as adventurous.

"Everyone else was in danger, except Extreme Cold." Running Elk released my hand and propped himself up on his elbow, his head resting in his palm.

I resisted the release at first then let go, hoping he'd soon shift positions and take my hand again in his. I felt hollow without his touch.

"The People were troubled by Extreme cold because he came during every season and they never knew when. So the chief called council to try and regulate the seasons. The People could not reach the lodge of Cold so they called South Wind, a medicine man of great power, to attack him. South Wind traveled north and ran into Extreme Cold. To South Wind's amazement, everything in front of him had perished. When Extreme Cold met South Wind, he tried to exercise his power, but nothing happened. No one had ever been able to withstand him.

Instead, South Wind addressed Extreme Cold as his nephew, telling him he lived in the south and that Northern Lights was his sister. He asked the way to his sister's lodge. Extreme Cold agreed to lead him there."

"Sounds like a trap," I said.

Running Elk leaned over and entwined my fingers in his. He gently rubbed my hand with his thumb.

I tightened my grip. Eyes closed, I smiled and prayed he'd love me enough to want my hand in marriage. This plan had to work. It was the only way to escape my folks' suffocating grasp. I opened my eyes to his voice, giving him a sideways glances as he told the legend.

"When they reached the ice lodge, Extreme Cold was full of steam. They went inside and South Wind claimed to be family. Northern Lights did not recognize him. She allowed him to stay the night with the plan to freeze him while he slept. The Cold family fell asleep so South Wind gathered pitch wood and set it on fire. The lodge and the Cold family thawed and perished in the flames. The seasons, as you call it, Hannah, were then regulated."

I thought about the story for a while. "The story seems to imply that lying is good."

"*Loot*," said Falling Rain. "It says to not let the enemy in. Do not trust in those you do not know. Make them prove themselves."

"But didn't the lie regulate the seasons?"

"It could have been done without the lie." Running Elk rolled over and propped himself up on an elbow.

"Do you think we are lying?"

"In a way we are," Falling Rain said. "We did not have the strength to tell the truth and fight for what we believe in. We ran away."

"Do you feel like you can reason with your pa?" I said.

"*Kewa*." There was a new boldness in Falling Rain's voice.

"Then we should go back." As sleepy as I was, I made no attempt to move.

"Tomorrow." Running Elk stood. "After I check my snares."

Chapter 17

The following morning, trout jumped in the water behind the weir. Falling Rain scooped several into her net and carried them back to camp. She gutted and filleted the fish, stabbing them with sticks. After making a fire, she roasted the trout, slowly turning them. The smell made my mouth water. Juice dripped on the fire and sizzled. My stomach growled.

Sips of willow tea eased my soreness enough I was able to sit by the fire, breathing fairly easily. "That smells wonderful."

Falling Rain nodded.

I flinched at the sound of cracking twigs in the trees and prayed it wasn't the intruder. Who knew what kind of scoundrel stole another person's food. Soon Running Elk appeared. He held out three rabbits and two squirrels. I sighed. He dropped the rabbits by my side. I picked them up, fingering the soft fur which would make for good moccasin liners in the winter.

He staked out his horse, skinned the small game, and roasted chunks of meat. The juice sizzled. I licked my lips. We ravaged every morsel, knowing there would be more fish to get us home. Falling Rain boiled more willow bark for the journey back. I'd never known a better friend.

After our meal we packed camp. The pain was unbearable at times, but I supposed it could be worse, and as Pa always said, "It's a long ways from your heart."

I took a few more sips of tea and settled onto Moonie's back. The trip up the hill was slow and methodical. Running Elk seemed to take the path easiest for me, but was also the longest. My mind stuck on his unsaid statement. When we stopped to rest, I got him alone and had to ask. "You said before, 'We should,' we should what?" I wrung my hands, hoping he would say we would marry as soon as we got back.

His eyes lit up. "We should hold a race similar to this course up north with the *Spukanee* and *Kalispeliwho*. We could invite others, too."

I sucked in a breath. *A Race?* My body tensed and the pain came back full force. All affections for him dissipated. "Are you serious?" The words squeaked out like an out of tune fiddle.

"What were you thinking?" Running Elk reached out to hold my hand.

I clenched my jaw and slapped his hand away, gasped from the pain in my sides. I squeezed my eyes shut. "Leave me alone!"

He sighed. "Talk to me. What did I do wrong?"

Nothing but a moan released from my tight throat as I doubled over.

Falling Rain rushed to my side. "What happened?"

"A race!" I said between clenched teeth.

"Running Elk, what happened?"

"I do not know!" he said. "She asked me a question and I answered her."

Falling Rain pointed to the horses. "Go!"

"What did I do?" He stalked off.

"I told him I wanted to marry him. All he can think about is racing!"

"We will talk about this later. We need to bind you." After shredding one of my shirtwaists, she bound my ribs and helped me back on my horse.

With a confused and hurt look on his face, Running Elk led the way. He was like every other brainless fella, and I was certain he was creating the perfect course for his new race as we rode across the mountain, despite my broken heart.

After a few hours, Running Elk glanced at me. "We will stop here and rest."

He must have seen the bitter look on my face and mistaken it for pain. We halted close to a pond. It looked clear and clean. I unscrewed my canteen lid and drank the last few drops of tepid metal-tasting water. My parched tongue soaked it up, begging for more. Falling Rain handed me her deer bladder, and I took a sip. "I don't need to rest."

Falling Rain grunted. "Sit." She pointed to the ground.

I slid off Moonie with a deep moan. It hurt to sit. It hurt to lie down. It hurt to stand and walk. I lay back with my knees up. That wasn't as miserable.

"There are huckleberries over there. I will go and get some." Falling Rain spun her horse around and trotted off.

I looked beyond her and caught a glimpse of movement far away. I stared until he came into view. A boy riding a ratty-tailed appaloosa peeked out from behind the trees. When he saw me looking his way, he ducked back, brush hiding his presence.

"Why are you following us?" I yelled loud enough for him to hear me.

"Who are you talking to?" Running Elk hovered over me.

I pointed to the trees. "Him."

Standing Bear rode into the clearing, eyes narrowed. Knife in hand, he pointed it at me. If I'd felt like it, and as much as he'd hassled me the last few months, I would have jumped to my feet and walloped him a good one.

"Stay by me," Running Elk said.

I shot him a scowl as if he told me to go cower behind a rock. I staggered to my feet, winced at the pain, and slumped back over, hugging myself.

Standing Bear reined his horse to a stop in front of us. He narrowed his eyes, staring right at me. "Because of Spupaleena my father is no longer a man. She stole that from him."

"She robbed him? Or did he hand her his manhood?" I stood straighter, one hand resting on Running Elk's shoulder.

He grunted. "I will punish her."

"So you keep saying." Perhaps it was the pain wracking my body that fogged my impressions, but I couldn't seem to take him seriously. To his surprise, and mine, I burst out laughing. Running Elk stared at me, open mouthed. I doubled over, laughed, choked, cried out in pain. And held my ground. I clutched my sides and took shallow breaths, trying not to laugh. "I reckon next you'll accuse me of stealing yours." I moaned from deep inside my throat.

"I'm coming for you. When you are not watching, I will get you!" Standing Bear spun his horse around and sped away.

I searched the woods, certain Wind Chaser was with him. Those two seemed inseparable—Standing Bear doing all the dirty work.

"What was that all about?" Running Elk held my shoulders.

His calloused hands scraped me like his calloused heart. I managed to slide to the ground and lay on my back, trying to find a position that caused the least amount of discomfort. Wind Chaser, even if not with Standing Bear, had to have coaxed him into following us. Coward!

Running Elk sat beside me and combed his fingers through his loose hair. "What did I say that upset you?"

I scooted my feet closer to my backside, relieving some of the soreness. I swallowed the lump in my throat. "I thought you were going to tell me that once we returned home, we would wed."

He looked away.

Never before had I wanted Falling Rain to hurry and come back. Now that the words were out, I felt exposed, fearing the contrary. Mama told me a few years back not to hurry love. Let it grow and bloom like a well-tended flower. And here I was, pushing, rushing, nearly begging. Afraid he changed his mind. Aunt Erma sounded favorable.

"I want to be with you." He leaned over and kissed my forehead. "I thought you knew. "I have loved you from the moment I first saw you. Not the little girl with pigtails riding her pony and chasing Spupaleena around," he smiled, "but the woman you have become." He ran his lips over the back of my hand.

His touch ignited sparks through me. "You do?" I tried not to sound desperate.

"I wish for us to wed." His voice sounded dejected. "It is not so simple."

I searched his face. "Why not?"

Running Elk took a long pause. "My father has arranged my marriage. That is why I wanted to run away with you. I fear now, when we return, his anger will…" He shook his head.

"Will what?" My tummy turned over like rocks in an eddy, scraping and ripping. I could not imagine what his pa would do. Beat him? Send him away? Ban me from the village? I reined in my runaway thoughts and studied his expression.

He had a faraway look about him. It resembled defeat. "I fear he will send me away. With her."

"We can stand together and fight…for us." I squeezed his hand. "Who is she?"

"Father won't change his mind." With tears in his eyes, he jumped to his feet and jogged away.

"Come back!" I lifted my body to stand, barely off the ground, and cried out in pain, trying to catch my breath. I fought to catch my breath as tears dripped down my face. I had to go after him. Convince him to live out here with me where we could remain together forever. Send Falling Rain home.

A strong, familiar hand touched my shoulder. Someone stood beside me and placed my canteen to my mouth. The cool wet taste touched my parched lips and tongue. It slid down my throat, too quickly. I coughed.

Running Elk pulled me into his arms.

I sobbed as he cradled me. I wanted him to love me so badly it hurt.

"We will find a way." He stroked my hair.

I relaxed in his embrace. *We will find a way.* I hung on to his promise. My tears soon dried up and I was able to sip more willow bark tea. But a heaviness in my heart lingered. "We can stay here."

"*Loot.* We will go and fight," Running Elk said. "It is time I stand for what I love and want. There are some traditions worth holding onto and others need to change."

He helped me lie back down, my head in his lap. Exhaustion consumed me, but my mind wouldn't let me sleep. I tried to focus on the sounds in the woods instead of the accusing thoughts running rampant throughout my head. As dusk hovered over the mountains, I got up. The air felt cold and damp. I shivered under a blanket, craving warmth. I craned my neck and saw Running Elk and Falling Rain hunkered down with their hands over a crackling fire, whispering. Without thinking, I rolled over and stood. Stabbing pain dropped me to my knees. I was certain binding my ribs hadn't made a difference.

Running Elk ran to my side and helped me shuffle to the fire. He sat me beside Falling Rain who handed me a cup of tea. I gulped the tepid liquid. Neither glanced my way and that was fine with me. I had nothing to say. In fact, the more I thought about Running Elk and his future bride, the angrier I got. Who was she? He never did answer.

I tossed a stick in the fire. It sparked and spit and sizzled. Sap stuck to my hand. I picked at it. I wanted to scream. I felt like the fire—spittin' mad. Without much thought I turned to Running Elk. "I don't care if your pa thinks another woman is fit for your hand in marriage. I'm the one that'll take care of you." I sucked in a breath and continued. "I don't see any reason we can't get married the minute we get back. No more hiding our feelings. It's time to stand up and fight for us!"

I turned back to the fire and threw in another pitched-filled hunk of wood. The sparks flew, making us all jump back. I hugged my ribs, struggling for air.

A look of shock covered Running Elk's face. Once I calmed down, he began to laugh. And so did Falling Rain. They laughed so hard it riled me up enough to struggle to my feet. I headed to my horse. The only faithful companion I had left. Who never laughed at me after I'd sliced open my heart and bared my deepest desires. I was intent on climbing my way into the saddle and leaving them sittin', carrying on like fools.

Running Elk stopped laughing enough to sit me back down. He knelt in front of me. "I will marry you. We can have children. Live where ever you want." He stared into my eyes. "You stand up for what you believe in. You give us," he motioned to Falling Rain with his chin, "a reason to fight for our desires." He took my hand in his. "*Kewa*. I will marry you the moment we get back."

I examined every inch of his thin face, from his big, round eyes to his crooked teeth. Was this real? We were really gonna get hitched? *What will Pa say?* An image of him cleaning his Sharps rifle wiggled into my mind.

Chapter 18

Fury sparked Pa.

The three of us stood in the rain wet, tired, and as hungry as a starved fox. Pa yelled at us for running away, for worrying the entire village. Somehow I didn't think that was true, considering most of them were in the mountains. Besides, the boys and half of the girls hated me for racing. Apparently Pa and Jack had stewed in Skumheist's lodge the entire time they'd been there. I assumed Pa already made a plan to hogtie and drag me back home. Or to Montana. Or farther yet. The threat of a girls' school back east swirled in my mind.

Spupaleena grabbed me by an arm before I had a chance to defend myself and shoved me inside her lodge. Her face was beet red. She tossed dry clothing at me that Mama sent over with Pa. "I do not know why you are so defiant." She snarled at me like a badger, pupils barely visible. She struck her hand with the handle of a horse whip as she paced.

I eyed that whip as I slipped on dry underclothing. I was certain she considered the use of it on my backside. "I'm old enough to make my own decisions." I tried to keep my voice calm and soft through gritted teeth.

She spun around. "Old enough?" She held her whip

inches from my nose. "If you were my child I would use this on you."

I went to turn my backside to her, but thought better of it. If she was gonna strike me, I wanted to see it coming. I slipped on a dry skirt and shirt waist. I blinked at Spupaleena, biting my tongue. "I'm sorry." The words squeaked out like a rabbit caught in a snare. "My intentions were not to worry anyone."

"They never are!" Spupaleena kept pacing, whip tapping her palm. "We cannot consider you a woman if you cannot behave like one."

Darn if she didn't have a point. "That is true." There was no use in me quarreling. No one ever won an argument with Spupaleena. I pulled on a boot. "When did Pa and Jack ride in?" I laced with aggression.

"Two days ago." She grunted. "They had not known you ran away from Delbert until my father told them you had been here. And then went missing, along with Running Elk and Falling Rain."

I shoved my other foot into a boot, jerking the laces tight. "Why are they here?"

"They wanted to talk with my father about fishing at the Kettle Falls for salmon during chokecherry picking season." Spupaleena poured a small amount of cooled red cedar tea over my scalp and ran her fingers through the tangles, jerking my head backward.

Chokecherry picking season was the month of September. The Sinyekst dried the berries for patties or mixed with meat to make pemmican.

I winced against her harsh movements. "Pa and Jack want to fish with your father?"

"Why does that surprise you? They have fished together before." Spupaleena found a brush, and this time she was gentler.

A sideways glance revealed the brush rested next to the whip. I interlaced my fingers so I wouldn't toss it outside, just in case she had a notion to use it on me.

Running Elk's father shouted outside Spupaleena's lodge, making me jump. I sprang to my feet, rushed through the tule flap, and stood by my future husband's side. No one was about to stop me from being Mrs. Running Elk. I reached for his hand, but he jerked it away. My heart dropped to the ground. Spupaleena stepped over and stood by my side, Pekam to her right.

Bird Caller's round belly jiggled with each word. "*Loot*! You will go live with my sister and her Spukanee husband if you cannot abide by my rules."

Running Elk stood tall, glaring at his father. "I am a man. Able to choose my own wife." He grabbed my wrist and held it up like I was some kind of trophy. "I want her."

I eyed Bird Caller, not real certain I wanted him to be my father-in-law. His temper scared me, made me question if he'd ever haul off and smack me. My knees knocked. Pa and Jack approached. I thought Pa'd stick up for me until I got a good look of his face.

Pa leaned on his walking stick, eyes flashing, nostrils flared. "Grab your things. We're leavin'."

Spurs jangling, Jack stepped behind me as if I'd run. His tall, slim body towered over mine. His black Stetson and red kerchief around his neck made him look like a bandit. I opened my mouth to protest when Jack grunted with a low, deep sound. I kept my gaze forward, wondering how he knew I was about to spout off.

I grabbed Running Elk's arm and held on for dear life, fighting the urge to vomit. Between my torn heart and the excruciating pain in my sides, I felt faint. "I will not go." I turned to Pa. "You and Mama tell me to settle down and find a husband. Well, I found one. And we plan to wed." With wobbling legs, I gazed at my beau and gasped at his blazing red face. I wasn't certain if it was anger, fear, or embarrassment that caused his face to color like it had. And I wasn't about to ask. I had to believe he loved me.

Our fathers tried to pull us apart. With a cry of pain, I clung to Running Elk's arm like a wolf to fresh meat. Running Elk curled his arm as if to support me. When we wouldn't give in, they let go. Running Elk remained by my side, and I sighed with relief and released my choke hold. But only enough to let my blood circulate. Everyone stared at me like I'd gone mad. So in case they didn't hear me the first time, bent over and struggling for air, I again stated my intensions. "We plan to wed!"

With those four words, chaos broke out like the Civil War. Bird Caller yelled in his Sinyekst tongue, talking so fast I couldn't catch his words. He pointed to Running Elk, Pa, and Jack. With his face as purple as storm clouds, he shook a fist at me. Pa shouted back, and Jack shoved me aside to defend his partner. I stumbled backward, clutching Running Elk's shirt.

"Come on!" I tried to pull my husband-to-be away from everyone, when strong hands grabbed me around my shoulders and held me captive. My body was too numb to feel sharp pain.

"Stay put," Pekam said with a snarl in his voice.

Pa took a crooked step in front of Bird Caller and shoved him aside with his walking stick.

"Enough!" Jack and his oversized boots stepped in between the two fathers, hands out to his sides. Bird

Caller looked as though he was not about to back down, even though his face came to Jack's chest. Clenched jaw and hands fisted, he planted his feet.

I tore away from Pekam and hobbled toward Moonie. With held breath, I untied my bow from the saddle and slung the quiver over my shoulder.

"Stop!"

I pressed the inside of my elbows to my sides as if that'd ease the sawing pain then lifted a leg to mount. "Oww!" Strong hands pulled me off and held me tightly around the waist. I flailed like a trapped hen.

"Stop fighting me," Pekam said.

The pain was too strong to continue. I went limp in his arms, struggling to catch a breath, sobbing. Pekam handed me off to Jack, who carried me to Spupaleena's lodge as if I were a fragile doll. When Spupaleena fumed in, Jack skedaddled, his face a mix of concern and rage.

"Stay here until I come for you." Spupaleena turned and followed Jack.

Chapter 19

Spupaleena came for me five days later. I had lain in her lodge with Smilkameen and Falling Rain hovering over me like a couple of mother bears. I was ready to get out and stretch my legs. My ribs were nearly healed, the purple fading to a dirty yellow. It was time to ride.

Clearly, Running Elk and I had no future. Not once during those five days did he come and see me. That gave me plenty of time to think about racing—without him. Obviously, he was not a suitable husband to help carry out my plan. I slid Delbert's trousers on and hung my pouch around my neck.

Pa and Jack were still here, and it was time to prove I was as fine a rider as Spupaleena had been at my age. I had one last chance and I was taking it while they were both here to watch me ride. If I failed, I'd surrender and go home.

I tugged my Stetson over my eyes like a bandit, strolled outside, and peered around. Pa, Jack, and Skumheist were on the edge of the tree line east of Spupaleena's lodge. Looked as though they were mending fishing nets. They had the perfect spot to watch me. I eyed a few trees as targets then saddled Moonie. There was no time to set up a course with leaves stuck to sticks.

I rode out several yards, looking back to see if Pa was watching. He was. I reined her around to face him. He stood and leaned against a tree for support.

I kicked Moonie into a lope, praying her gait would be smoother than usual. Head up and eyes forward, I searched for the first target. I drew the first arrow, fit it to the bow, and pulled back. I wrapped my legs around Moonie's body to steady my aim. "Easy, girl." With a held breath and reins looped around the saddle horn, I released the arrow. It plunged into the center of a tree knot.

My trembling fingers fumbled for the second arrow. I pulled it out, finding the next target. My gaze spotted a squirrel in a tree and I released the arrow. It was sheer luck for this greenhorn to pierce that squirrel smack in the middle. That or the Good Lord decided to grace me with a pinch of favor.

I searched west for a target opposite the men so I wouldn't accidentally stick them with my arrow. The only thing in view was my sweetheart and his stumpy father. As tempted as I was, I surged past Pa and the others, finding a third target on the east side of the narrow meadow. A sap bulge caught my eye. I hit two more targets for good measure, circled Moonie around, and slid her to a stop between the onlookers.

My stunned soon-to-be father-in-law stood with his mouth agape. He resembled an overripe huckleberry. At this point, I'd either proved my womanhood or pierced my spirit and was headed home. Fear kept my gaze from Pa. Instead I gave Jack a sideways glance, knowing he could do something like that with his eyes closed. As expected, a sly grin crossed his face. I held back a smile as my focus rolled toward Pa. It fell on his boots, toes tapping. I lifted my lashes and saw pride wrestlin' with fury.

"I gotta stay." I choked on the words then shifted my gaze to Running Elk.

Running Elk's face beamed with pride. Until Calling Bird shoved him toward the village, shouting curse words in his own language. "Blossom" and "wife" were two of the many words he bellowed at his son. I knew of Blossom. She was hardworking, traditional, soft spoken, and tall. A tall and slender tule stalk dancing in a gentle breeze. I'd seen her dance around the fire at the first roots ceremony a few years back. Her body flowed as smooth and elegant as a butterfly.

I feared, after Running Elk may have talked his father into allowing our nuptials, I'd just ruined it. Why else would they have come to speak with us? I took hold of my honey-colored braid and moaned. I was nothing more than an under-developed twig—faded, scared, twirling in the wind, circling the village and going nowhere. Never could I be as lovely as Blossom. She was everything a man like Bird Caller desired in a daughter. Hardworking, soft-spoken, attractive, obedient, and, of course, Indian.

I dismounted and handed Jack the reins. Running Elk looked over his shoulder and snagged my attention, horror struck his eyes. I took a step toward him, but Pa pressed an arm to my elbow. "Let's take a walk." He led me down the meadow. We stopped under a grove of aspen and sat in its shade. He leaned against the white bark, laying his walking stick beside him—closest to me. He pulled a blade of grass and slid it between his teeth. I reckoned he was chewing on what to say. I hugged my knees and waited. I had no defense. I was guilty of running away—more than once. Scripture said to forgive.

And that's what I counted on—forgiveness and grace.

"I'm sorry, Pa." I had to speak before I burst.

He shook his head. "You've always been a spitfire." He stretched his legs out, rubbing his stump. The wooden peg Jack had made for him years ago looked old and faded. Almost splintered. Worn like Pa.

I lay my cheek on my knees with my face toward him. "Can't dispute that."

He studied me like he normally did before touching an unbroken colt. "Why Running Elk?"

All the reasons swam across my mind like the salmon that traveled upriver to spawn. "He's kind and gentle. Treats me right. Like you treat Ma. He has strong ranching skills and ideas." I picked a blade of grass and chewed on it, letting its sweet flavor rinse the bitterness from my mouth. I fingered the canoe. *Listen to Pa. Listen to the Lord. Forget them! Listen to your heart.*

Pa grunted. "Ranchin' or racin'?"

"Both, I reckon." I wished I'd had on a skirt. It was hard to act like a lady in men's britches. Especially my brother's. I picked at the fabric.

"You steal those from your brother?"

I swallowed hard. "Yeah. They were under my skirt the morning we left."

"Delbert go on to the Spukanee village?"

"How'd you know?"

"I got my ways, child."

Child. That stung. Relaxed, I noticed the ache in my sides. I hugged my ribs, not about to complain.

"What's the matter with you?"

"I want you to believe in me." Tears welled in my eyes as I thought about how he used to convince Ma to let me race when I was a little girl. I looked away. What made him change his mind? We used to laugh together. Worked cattle side by side. That job shifted to Delbert while I was stuck in the house daydreaming about being outside with the boys, working the ranch.

He pointed to my side. "I meant, why are you breathing like that?"

"A little sore is all."

"Why would you be sore? What went on out there?"

I was surprised he didn't know I got hurt. Perhaps part of my punishment, as I'm certain was at Spupaleena's insistence, was I tell him on my own.

"Don't you be keeping no secrets from me, child."

Child? He made me want to scream! One minute they want me to mature and the next they won't let go. I wished they'd make up their minds.

"Hannah?" His voice softened. "Did that boy hurt you? You know…"

"What? Hurt me? No!" I turned and sat on my knees, facing my pa, anger boiling inside like a hot kettle of kerosene. The twist of my body grabbed my ribs and I swear it felt as though they were splittin' in half. I squeezed my eyes shut, crying out in pain.

Pa held my arm. "Tell me."

I sighed. "I took a bad spill on Moonie when we were practicing for the shooting race." I pulled out the last of my willow bark and chewed on it. My mouth was so dry it took a bit to get any saliva pooled, but when it did, the juice slid down my throat and my body relaxed. I leaned against the tree.

"Let me take a look." He reached for my shirtwaist.

I batted his hand out of the way. "I'm fine, Pa. Really,

I am." A rush of embarrassment flew up my neck, not to mention added discomfort. "Smilkameen's been treatin' me with her medicine."

He held up his hands in surrender.

The worry in his eyes as he stared across the meadow scooped out a hole in my gut. After some time, the silence between us gnawed at me. I did not know what he was pondering, but figured it included Aunt Erma. "Pa, I can't go to Montana." Enough reasons why spun in my head, but they wouldn't stop long enough for me to flush them out my mouth.

"I think it's best. Now that you've run away with a boy," he shook his head, "what are folks gonna say?" He turned his head away from me.

"But nothing happened. And we weren't alone," I pleaded. "We had Falling Rain chaperone. He never laid a hand on me." I wasn't about to tell him he'd kissed me. Or how it made my insides flutter.

"It doesn't matter. You were together." He sighed. "You don't tend to think things through, only do whatever stirs your emotions and only later realize the consequences." He picked at the blade of grass that'd been in his mouth. "That's not the actions of a responsible woman. We expect more from you. Being the oldest and all."

I held back a sob.

A tear trickled down his face. "I can't be worryin' about you."

"If you send me to Montana, I'll never come back. You know I won't." I stood, glaring at the man I loved, my heart torn to pieces. With no reply from Pa, I stomped away.

Chapter 20

Three distraught families sat outside Skumheist's lodge. Calling Bird crossed his arms—his grimace bored through me—causing my skin to crawl. Running Elk slumped beside him, eyes cast down. His expression made me wonder if he'd settled for Blossom.

I sat between Jack and Pa, still looking like a prisoner. I was astonished they hadn't yet shackled me. I had a notion it was coming. My emotions told me to act fast. But Pa's harsh words, calling me "child," kept me planted on the log all three of us squatted on.

Pekam sat in the middle of the horseshoe-shaped semi-circle, squirmin' like an impatient child.

Pa tapped the dirt with his walking stick. I wanted to grab the darn thing and toss it in the river. It would have pleased me to watch it float downstream. Earlier, I'd slid my canoe in my pocket. To keep my mouth shut, I rubbed the smooth wood. We waited for Spupaleena as if she were the judge and we were on trial. Things seemed mighty dismal. I caught Running Elk's gaze. His blank-looking eyes made contact with mine for a brief moment before shifting his focus into the woods. My heart cracked as he slipped through my fingers. It left a gaping hole.

Spupaleena bustled over and sat beside Pekam. He settled down. My stomach rolled over like whitecaps on a stormy day. Spupaleena nodded to her father. She had a peace about her that made me sit up. Mares and foals raced by behind us, boys on ponies chasing them.

Once the pounding hoof beats faded, Skumheist spoke. "This has been a difficult time for many." He glanced at Running Elk and me.

My face grew hot, but I held my position—chin level, eyes on Skumheist. Like the Sinyekst warriors in the village, I needed to look fear in the face.

"Words have been said," Skumheist continued. "Some true and some with a lying tongue. We have to discover the truth. This is the way of our people. Running Elk claims he did not soil Hannah, and I believe him. As does his father."

My focus darted to Running Elk, to Calling Bird, to my father, and to the ground. My shoulders slouched, wishing Falling Rain was beside me.

Skumheist held my gaze. "Falling Rain's father also confirmed this as witnessed by his daughter."

I nodded and again sat straight, trying to pass myself off as confident and ladylike.

"I spoke with Elizabeth." Spupaleena watched me.

My gaze met hers. *So that's why I haven't seen her the last couple of days.* I shook my head, eyes narrow.

"We talked about Hannah's threats and rebellious ways." Spupaleena switched her focus to Pa.

"And I think we are all in agreement," Pa said.

Calling Bird grunted. "Running Elk will go live with our Spukanee family. He will leave in the morning."

"No!" I leaped to my feet and studied my future

husband's face.

Running Elk watched me with a cold, bitter stare. I shook my head, my eyes pleading with his.

Jack pulled me down. "It's the only way," he said in a low tone. "Calling Bird asked to have you banned from the village."

"Banned?" I couldn't drag my focus away from Running Elk. His expression switched to sorrow. Then I knew. I knew this wasn't what he wanted. Tears trickled down my face and I let them.

Calling Bird rose and spoke to his son and me with a harsh tone. Running Elk stood, turned, and walked away, his father trailing behind him. He had to have a plan. That's why he wasn't speaking. We had until the next morning. I heard them tell us—we had time.

I wanted to die. Right then and there. Confusion spun around me, squeezing my chest. I ripped away from Jack's grip and ran.

"Hannah, stop!" Pa said.

Hitched footsteps rushed behind me, making me run faster. "Leave me be, please!" I found Moonie, haltered her, and galloped off, riding bareback. Tears streaked down my face. *Maybe I should have gone to Montana.*

Hours later, I reined Moonie to a halt. We'd covered miles of ground, and at some point, turned east into territory I hadn't yet explored. It was time to turn back. The moon would be hanging high by the time I'd arrive back at the village. My stomach growled and I realized I'd skipped two meals. I scrounged and found a handful of huckleberries. They only made my mouth dry and sticky. I kicked Moonie into a trot, not wanting to face anyone.

Could they not see how much we loved each other? I was convinced Calling Bird was blind. Blinded by his own pride. Pa was just plain stubborn. Running Elk and I had plans—a life carved out that included children and ranching. We could have split our time between the two families.

In the morning.

There was still time. Somehow, some way, I had to do something to change Calling Bird's mind. But what?

CHAPTER 21

When I returned to the village it was quiet. Too quiet. Eerie fingers wrapped around me like a blanket. Sweat mixed with dust covered my hands and arms. I wiped them on my britches, not caring how dirty I was. Birds chirped in the distance. Their joy made me want to ring their necks. *Chirp, chirp, chirp*. I stripped off the saddle and walked Moonie to the river. Wind Chaser sneered at me as I strode past him. After Moonie had her fill of river water and cooled off, I moseyed back to Spupaleena's lodge.

Pa sat on a log outside Skumheist's lodge, whittling. "Running Elk's gone."

"When?" I said with a hitch in my voice.

"Not long ago. He wanted to talk to you before he left. Calling Bird only allowed him to wait so long. I offered to relay a message, but..."

I dropped to the ground and sobbed. I mourned the loss of friendship, of love. Not a mindless scheme but real love. I cried over my family's disappointment in me, mine in them. I had no inkling how we'd ever repair the damage. I could only pray. I released the sorrow and broken dreams. Finally spent, I looked up. "I reckon we're headed home in the morning?"

Pa laid his wood and knife on the ground. "Before you return, Spupaleena will take you in the mountains. She planned to tell you the news before you ran off. She figured you need time to decide what path you wanna follow. I'll stay with Skumheist and fish."

"What did Ma tell Spupaleena?"

Pa rubbed his gnarled knuckles. "I suppose she trusts the Lord and Spupaleena enough to allow you start making decisions on your own." He sighed. "She's tired of fighting you." Pa removed his Stetson and rubbed his brow with his forearm.

"I'm sorry, Pa. I never meant to cause such a commotion." I fought back tears. "I meant to show you that I am in control of my life."

Pa paused before stating, "Is it you who should be in control?"

I gulped. "I reckon not."

"Is there even a scrap of Him in your life?" He settled his hat back on his head.

I glanced away. "Reckon not much."

"And how is that workin' for ya?" Pa smiled.

I knew he was tryin' to lighten the air between us. "Not so well." He had a gentle way of putting me in my place. Pa was a man of peace, like scripture read: It's better to be peaceful than to quarrel. Too bad his peace could not mend my broken heart.

The following morning, the hour the sun painted the sky a pale orange, I headed out with Spupaleena and two other women. One of the women led a packhorse with food and supplies. They all had bows and quivers slung over their backs as did I. Part of me ran wild with anticipation, the other part hung back, heavy with grief. The two kept fighting inside me, so I prayed the Lord would settle them down, replacing them with…well, I rightly didn't know with what.

We rode east, over the mountains and swerved south. Past the loons and back to Frosted Meadows. It took most of the day. We set up camp and tethered the old pack horse. He seemed glad for the rest and went to munching yellow grass, stretching his neck for the greener blades closest to the water.

I'd learned the other two women's names along the trail. The taller one with the long, thin face was Spotted Fawn. The shorter one, a fist taller than Spupaleena, with a round face and happy eyes, was Glowing Moon. Spotted Fawn had lost her husband the previous summer. She wouldn't talk much about him, and Spupaleena warned me not to ask questions, as she knows my curious ways.

Glowing Moon's husband raced horses, too. She said *Koolenchooten* hadn't given them children yet and until then, nothing would get in her way of racing. I didn't think because she popped out a young'n or two meant she gotta quit. The Sinyekst supported one another. I figure a cousin or auntie could watch the little bugger a time or two, here and there.

Spupaleena shared how the three of them made a fine relay team. Glowing Moon normally held the first horse and Spotted Fawn clung onto the second, which was taller and spunkier. Even though her height and strength made handling him easier, she said her hands got rope burned pretty badly the first time. It took many days to heal. After that she wore buckskin gloves and learned to use her body weight to anchor her feet to the ground.

Made me glad I was a rider and not a handler.

"It has been a long journey today. The horses can rest while we gather firewood, eat, and shoot bows," Spupaleena said.

"Think this little one can handle her bow?" Glowing Moon ran a finger down the yew wood, seemingly impressed.

I laughed. "Hope you don't lose your arrow."

The women giggled, making a few more jokes.

"Your niece likes to use her words. She is clever," Glowing Moon said in Sinyekst.

I picked up a few sticks and pine cones for the fire. "Not bad for a greenhorn."

"What is a greenhorn?" Spotted Fawn said.

"Someone with little or no savvy under their hat." I pointed to my head.

Spotted Fawn gave me a quizzical look, peering under my Stetson. She gave me what sounded like a gracious laugh. Somewhere between I still don't fully understand, and I'm trying really hard to not hurt your feelings. She shrugged and went on to gather deadfall.

I shot Spupaleena a sideways eye roll. She chuckled.

After gathering firewood, we met at the west edge of the meadow. Spotted Fawn stuck several aspen leaves to the bark of a tamarack with sap. We each had ten arrows. I hoped I'd be able to find them all before dark.

Spotted Fawn shot first. She used three arrows and hit all three leaves. After retrieving her arrows, Glowing Moon shot three arrows, and then Spupaleena shot. All three hit the leaves. My turn came. Sweat-soaked palms clutched my bow. The air cool, perspiration trickled down my back.

I felt their eyes on me. They stepped back farther than necessary, as if teasing I'd need the room. I fixed my arrow to the bow string, thinking about Falling Rain's instructions. Both eyes open, I aimed and pulled back. I told myself this was for pleasure. My body ignored me and shook like the leaves in a stiff breeze. Whispers from behind me floated to my ears. My attention lobbed back and forth from their voices to the target.

I opened my fingers and as the arrow hit the tree, bark flying. I missed the leaf, but not by much. Someone clapped behind me—figured it was my auntie. Mama had taught her to clap at our successes. I tugged a second arrow out of the quiver and took aim, pulling the string back as far as I could.

"You will hit it this time, greenhorn," Glowing Moon said, her voice loud and confident.

I tried to remain straight-faced. The way she said greenhorn sounded like greenmourn. I drew in a deep breath and held it. Aimed. Released. The arrow nicked the edge of the leaf.

"Awww, she hit it." Glowing Moon stepped up to the tree and examined the leaf. "I need one of those looking glasses your friend Jack has."

Spotted Fawn chuckled. I swiveled around to affirm it was her. Her face shone, something I'd not yet witnessed from her. It brightened me.

Glowing Moon patted my shoulder as she sashayed back to the others. "You will get it this time. I can feel it in the air."

"You can?" I was fascinated with how well she was in tune with nature.

"I can feel it, too." Spotted Fawn held her hands up to the heavens and wiggled slender fingers.

Spupaleena joined in with one finger up in the air. "The wind tells me you will not only hit *naux*, but also *aseel, Kook Yuma Mahooya*."

"Twice? Really?" I grunted at them and faced the tree. "Watch me hit this leaf." I had a notion they were playing with me.

I fixed a third arrow to my bow and pulled back. I made certain the tip of the arrow was pointed dead center at the leaf. I let loose and closed my eyes. I couldn't look this time, fearing I would again miss. Within a second or two I heard bark spray. With eyes squeezed tightly, I scrunched my nose.

War whoops echoed off the hills as the women behind me cheered and chanted. I opened my eyes and turned to see them beating sticks in the palm of their hands. I giggled and twirled around, hands raised above my head, stopping to face the tree. The arrow stuck in the leaf, not in the center, but in far enough to make it count. I danced around, mimicking the sounds the women made. I was one of them. Accepted into their tribe. And it felt pleasing. It made me forget about Wind Chaser, Running Elk, and Blossom, if only for a little while.

"Tomorrow you will shoot while riding Moonshine," Spupaleena said. "You can show us how much skill you have."

Running Elk never missed his mark off a horse. How tall and handsome he looked while doing so. His bright smiles and easy eyes. They made my tummy flutter. Why hadn't he fought harder? Perhaps he loved Blossom after all.

That night the stars tapped the heavens as I lay awake, unable to sleep. "Lord, please bring Running Elk back to me."

Chapter 22

After a fistful of cold bannock and dried salmon I saddled my mare.

Spupaleena unsaddled her. "You cannot ride as one with a saddle in between." She set my saddle on a log and slapped the horse blanket on top. "No more." She took a few steps back and turned to me. "And from now on you talk our language. No more English. Your Sinyekst needs to improve."

My stomach from last night intensified. *What if I fall off? What if they laugh at me?*

"You talk big, but the look on your face shows fear. Moonie can sense that and will not like it." Spupaleena walked away. "Enough playing. Time to get serious," she said over her shoulder.

I tried to figure out Spupaleena's brisk change of mood while I bridled Moonie. At times she acted more like my mama than my mentor. What was wrong with having pleasure woven in with training? The three of them sat on their horses and waited, staring at me, hiding grins as they bit their lips.

By the time I wiggled onto my horse's back, they'd ridden several yards away. Glowing Moon trotted up to Spotted Fawn, passing her a stick. In turn, Spotted Fawn trotted to Spupaleena and passed the stick. Looked like game playing to me. My aunt confused me. Were we playing games or training?

I kicked Moonie into a lope to catch up, sliding all over her back as if sitting atop a wet log. I was used to gripping the saddle horn for leverage. I caught myself repeatedly grabbing for something that was not there. I figured from my time riding bareback with Running Elk and Falling Rain, I'd be sturdier. Spupaleena was right—it was time to hone my bareback skills.

"You going to wear that skirt?" Glowing Moon said.

I glanced down, slipped off Moonie, and changed into Delbert's trousers. Apparently, pining over Running Elk was more of a distraction than I'd counted on. My belt was nowhere to be found. I pulled a piece of twine from my parfleche and cinched up my trousers, ignoring the women's snickers. I lifted my chin and wiggled back onto my mare.

We took the rest of the morning and practiced shooting our bows at any spoken target at a walk and trot. Spupaleena made the targets close to the ground—I'm certain in case I missed. My balance got better once I learned to hang on with my knees and not so much with my feet. As I sank into Moonie's back and relaxed, my shot improved. "I think we need to try knives." I smiled.

Spupaleena didn't give me the time of day. Then I realized I'd spoken English. A natural-born habit. So I asked in Sinyekst, patting the knife tucked away in my pocket.

Spupaleena nodded. "Get the hang of this and I will consider switching."

After a few more shots and after switching horses a couple times, we went into the mountains to pick huckleberries. Before we picked, the women taught me how to make a pine needle basket. Although it was lopsided, I was able to fill it with fresh berries before the sun went down.

We were about to head back to camp when Spotted Fawn put a finger to her lips. She gathered her bow and an arrow with a quiet and gentle and swift motion. With one shot we had fresh rabbit. She saved the pelt to line her moccasins come winter.

The smell of rabbit meat roasting on sticks wafted up my nose. My stomach rumbled. I popped a few huckleberries in my mouth and let the juice trickle down my throat. I took one of the sticks from Spotted Fawn and rotated the meat above the flames.

My mind drifted to Running Elk. I missed his touch. The smile that made his soft face look much younger than he was. I missed how his eyes glimmered when they locked onto mine. Chills ran up my arms and a tear slid down my cheek. I turned away so the others wouldn't see. Then the tears wouldn't stop. They rained down my face and the only thing I could do was to get up and walk away.

"Where are you going?" Spupaleena asked.

I could hardly think let alone choke out any words. "To relieve myself," was all I could muster. I waved the meat pierced stick and kept going. I rushed to the creek and walked until I found a quiet place and a tree I could lean against. I allowed myself to sob, realizing I would probably never see Running Elk again. I needed to admit it and move forward. I didn't know how I'd do that, especially with my heart ripped to shreds. Images of Spupaleena and the friends' disappointed looks glided into my mind. And Pa's face when he told me Running

Elk was gone. With reluctance I wiped my face and picked at the rabbit meat. I remained a little longer, listening to the creek trickle down the meadow before returning to the fire.

I sat beside Spupaleena, trying to hide my hurt, and ate the rest of the meat.

Spupaleena tossed her empty stick into the fire. "Were you ready to get married?"

I thought for a minute. "*Kewa.*" The Sinyekst word slipped out as though I'd was born speaking it. I bit my lip, fighting back tears.

"Were you ready for every part of marriage?" Spotted Fawn asked.

"What do you mean? I know how to cook and clean and care for children. Mama did a fine job of making sure I know how to take care of my future family." I had paid attention, learning in spite of my obsession with horses and ranch work with Pa and Delbert and Jack.

"That is not what I mean." Spotted Fawn glanced at Spupaleena.

Glowing Moon wagged a finger. "She means are you ready for relations with a man."

I gasped. "Oh…" I rubbed my eyes as smoke swirled by, stinging them. "Um…No…" I stirred the dirt with a rabbit roasting stick. I knew what they meant. Breeding horses taught folks early on in life. But I hadn't given it a thought.

"Have you thought of where and how you would live once married?" Spupaleena asked.

"We could live in the village. Or split our time between there and the cabin."

Glowing Moon grunted. "Do you think Running Elk

would agree to move from his people? And in with your folks?"

I opened my mouth to speak but was cut off.

"What would he do, herd cattle? Does he want to?" Spupaleena said.

I wrung my hands. Cold, hard reality sank in. "We never talked about any of it, really. We talked about raising and racing horses. You all do. Why can't we?"

"It is not as easy as you think," Spupaleena said.

My jaw dropped. "What? But…"

"I have always wanted to have a family. But no man wants me because I race. They want a wife who will raise children and follow unspoken village rules. I never wanted that until it was too late. I have given up everything because of my selfishness." Spupaleena tossed more sticks on the flames. "I have regrets."

I glanced at Spotted Fawn, wanting to ask her why she raced. Does she not want another family? I opened my mouth to ask then thought better of it.

She caught my gaze. "I miss my husband." She cleared her throat. "I wish he was here." She looked up to the heavens. "But *Koolenchooten* took him from me. I tried to take my own life." She showed me her wrists. "To help push away the pain, I began training with Spupaleena." A tear slipped down her face as she peered at Spupaleena. "My friend saved me. She gave me hope."

I stared at her scars. They were still thick and raised and red. Whys reeled through my mind, but no words could get past the lump in my throat. I turned to Glowing Moon. Without me asking, she offered her thoughts.

"I am one of the few married women who race. My husband and I agree that once we have children, I am finished. I am young—married for only a year now. It will not be long until I am ready to raise my family."

I shook my head. All these years I thought my auntie had the perfect life. But now her face only reflected sorrow. "Why don't you stop?"

"I am too set in my ways." Spupaleena gave me a sad-looking smile.

"It's not too late. Mama says it's never too late." I wondered who she had her eye on. Even though she was not admitting it, she'd told Mama there was someone she was interested in. My mind showered me with images of men in her village who had lost their wives. Men suitable for Spupaleena. One lost his wife in childbirth. Another from pneumonia last winter during a cold spell. Others from various illnesses.

"Have you considered the differences in traditions and beliefs?" Glowing Moon said. "My husband is of the *Kalispeliwho*, but we have similar beliefs. I do not think we would like each other if we quarreled all the time."

"I don't…"

"You have your religion, Running Elk has his own." Spotted Fawn gave me a soft smile. "Would you give up *Koolenchooten*?"

"No!" I spoke a little too quickly then softened. "I figured he'd choose mine."

"What if he wanted to keep his?" Spupaleena said. "Not all of us see *Koolenchooten* in the same way."

My heart sank deeper with every comment. It was clear I had not thought these nuptials through. "But you believe, Auntie."

"*Kewa.* I do believe in the Lord. But I also know Bird Caller does not, and I do not think Running Elk does either. He loved you, not your religion," Spupaleena said.

There was much I had not considered. I assumed Running Elk would live like me. Even if we stayed in the village, things may not have been like I thought or hoped for. Doubt flowed through me and an emptiness I'd never felt before settled inside me like a hollow log.

I had nothing more to say, so I went to bed. I stared at the stars and asked the Lord, "Why?" Crickets and birds spoke to me, but He remained silent.

Chapter 23

The following morning I walked along the creek. The Lord remained silent, but I think it was because He had already spoken through Spupaleena, Glowing Moon, and Spotted Fawn. The creek flowed past me. A healing current washed away my guilt, doubt, fears, and hurt. It may have been over with Running Elk, but I wasn't ready to give up on racing. I had to attempt a few more times. There was plenty of time to hunt for a husband.

With a lightened heart I hastened back to camp, eager for additional training. "What are we doing now?" I glanced around. Neither Spupaleena nor her horse were in sight.

"She went back," Glowing Moon said.

"Back where?" I glanced in the direction we'd come.

"To the village," Spotted Fawn said.

I frowned. "Why?"

Glowing Moon chuckled. "She knew you would protest."

I got nowhere with those two. "And what would I be protesting?"

"You riding back by yourself."

I figured they were teasing. "What are we doing next?"

"We are going berry picking. You are riding back to the village." Spotted Fawn rolled up her hide and tied it to her willow bark saddle. She placed one blanket on the horse, then the saddle, and finally a second blanket to cushion the wood for a more comfortable ride.

Only my belongings cluttered camp. Glowing Moon and Spotted Fawn mounted their horses and rode off without a good-bye or a wave. I assumed they were heading to their families in the hills. Moonie whinnied as the horses walked away. My tummy growled and it was then I panicked. I rushed to my pack and dug through it. Luckily, one of the women left me a handful of bannock and dried salmon. I ate the food in a state of self-pity. Would I remember the way home? Was this some kind of test?

For years Spupaleena told me stories of vision quests young Sinyekst took. Was this one of them? I glanced about the meadow and saw no movement. *Lord, I reckon it's you and me.* After filling my canteen with water, I saddled Moonie and headed out. I followed the sparse trail. Along the path I ran into a huge huckleberry patch. I rummaged around, found my basket, and started picking. I picked and placed in my basket and ate, picked and placed in my basket and ate.

It was hardly enough. My belly rumbled. In the distance twigs broke and brush rustled. Old legends of Sinyekst spirits roaming in the mountains spooked me. I tried to pray it away, but with each sound I became more and more rattled. The hair on my arms stood on end. A deer bounded out of the brush, and I fell backwards trying to spring to my feet. I knelt, studying each waving leaf and chirping noise. Who knew what kind of spooks patrolled this territory?

Something rustled in the brush to my right. I reached back and got my bow, fitting an arrow to the string. If this was a test or quest, I was determined to walk into the village with some sort of game. I crouched, closed my eyes, and listened. Squirrels chattered as if to make fun of me. Birds trilled and flitted about. Nothing happened for the longest time. My legs cramped, so I shifted positions, growing impatient.

A squirrel scampered up a big fir and as I aimed, he darted around the back of the tree. I held the bow at a draw and waited. Another squirrel came into view. I took aim and released the arrow.

To my surprise the arrow stuck the varmint to the tree. I jumped to my feet and retrieved my meal. *Eat it now or save it for later?* My hunger pangs won the battle. I slid my knife from my pocket and skinned it the best I knew how and slid chunks of meat on a stick. I leaned against a tree, realizing there was no flint to start a fire. So I did what any warrior would have done—took a bite of the stringy, blood-soaked meat and choked it down. Somehow I managed to eat the warm, raw meat without retching, even while bile climbed up my throat. A handful of berries in between bites helped sweeten my mouth and settle my tummy. Each chunk slid down a little easier than the previous.

I tied the bloody hide to my saddle horn in case I didn't find any more game, knowing Pekam would ask for proof. My patience wore thin after a long time of squattin' in the dirt with no critters showing their faces. With a stiff back and legs, I mounted Moonie and continued down the path. Thoughts of Running Elk swarmed me. One minute I was praying he'd find me. The next I was swearin' him off. At some point, my mind shifted to Wind Chaser. I asked myself how far he'd go to stop me. Was it worth it? For now it was.

I managed to make it back to Spupaleena's lodge by midday. A red-headed boy sat out front. I only know one boy with hair the color of fire. He fiddled with something in his hands.

"What are you doing here?" I said from Moonie's back.

"After finding out Ma and Pa knew you were here, I reckoned you needed someone to defend you." Delbert didn't look up of from his hunk of wood. A horse's head emerged from under his small pocketknife.

"Defend me?" Heat rose up my neck. "I can take care of myself. In fact, I had me a vision quest. Got a squirrel, skinned it, and ate it. Raw." I held out the tiny hide with crimson-stained fingers.

That made Delbert look up. He grunted and went back to whittling. "Those my britches?"

I believe he was so impressed his tongue got tied. I pictured him bitin' it so hard it bled. His lips were slightly pursed. That pleased me. "Sure are."

"You think you had a vision quest, huh?" He skinned a few slices of wood, exposing more of the horse. Pa gave him that knife when he turned eight. Got him using it as a little tyke, with supervision, of course. Now his craft was, I hated to admit, splendid. As good as the old-timers.

"I know I did." I slid off Moonie.

He laughed. Louder that I liked, and it made my blood boil. I fisted my hands and took a step toward him.

"Go cool off in the river," he said, "might clear your head." He kept his gaze on his work. He looked smug, leaning against his saddle, legs stretched out. I lifted my hand to grab that red hair of his, drag him down to the river, shove his face in… I shook my head and dropped my hand. I knew those desirable actions would not please our folks as it was less than ladylike. Instead, I spun on my heels and took Moonie to the river for a drink.

Chapter 24

My mouth was as dry and dusty as burnt wood. I pressed a hand to my empty stomach. I could not find Spupaleena, Pekam, or Skumheist anywhere. With the women in the mountains, I hesitated to ask the elder men for guidance. It did not seem proper. Mama talked about keeping with women as it was the more suitable behavior. I walked farther along, the sun low in the sky. Wind Chaser and his little brother played some kind of stick game in the distance. I pondered the notion of such kindness in the most evil boy I knew, hoping it was real.

My legs begged me to run and protect the scrawny brother. He looked to be five or so and was barefoot and dirt-covered. The smile on his face as he reached for Wind Chaser's hand stopped me. The brothers walked toward me, hand in hand, smiling and teasing. Laughing. I could not believe what I was witnessing.

Wind Chaser's face appeared soft, not the hard and twisted look he'd given me. But with striking features. Somewhat handsome. Enough to send shivers up my arms. My feet remained planted in the dirt as they came closer. The boy walked with a limp, one foot turned in and up. Wind Chaser kept his focus on his brother. They looked alike, both with big, round eyes and the same broad nose. Both with clefts in their chins. They strolled past me as if I did not exist.

I ignored my hunger pangs, followed, hanging back enough to remain invisible, and tied Moonie to a tree. Once by the shore, Wind Chaser picked up his brother and waded into the river, one cautious step at a time. This baffled me. I'd never seen him behave in such a gentle or loving manner. This was the boy who attacked me time after time. Who'd threatened me. And now, a side of him I thought never existed came forth.

I wondered if I was in some sort of trance from my vision quest. I sat in the shade of a tree, hugging my knees.

Wind Chaser splashed his brother as the boy tilted back his head, laughing so hard I thought he'd burst like an overripe berry squished between finger and thumb. He twirled his brother in slow, methodical circles, as if the boy would break. Then he stopped and looked up. Straight at me.

I froze.

His face hardened like a knotted stump, lips twisting like an angry bull. The boy stopped laughing and turned to me. He then turned said something to Wind Chaser, who shook his head, and turned his gaze back on me.

I jumped to my feet and grabbed Moonie. I watered her farther north before returning to Spupaleena's lodge. After placing my mare back in her corral, and still shook up, I rushed inside the lodge and banged my head on the entrance pole. With a groan, I plopped down on a tule-mat, rubbing my head. *Good Lord, what was I thinking? He'll always be as mean as a riled rattler.*

My tummy growled deep and low. I ransacked baskets and bags hanging from the lodge poles. A rough substance told me I'd found dried salmon. I pulled some out and shoved it between my lips. Between my sour mood and parched mouth, it tasted awful. I bent over to spit it out, then thought of how little food they sometimes had. With salmon in my mouth, I searched for water and found none. I dashed the short distance to my saddle, grabbed a canteen, and took a deep swig. I wiped my mouth and took another, leaning against the corral railing which held Moonie. I sighed, my gaze falling on Delbert.

He stared at me, opened mouth. His knife, tip up and in his hand, rested on his lap. "You eat some kind of poison to make you go crazy?"

I sneered at him. Took another drink, walked back to the lodge, and slipped inside. I had me a vision and now I was suddenly irrational? It was real. It had to be. Or maybe it was simply the Lord speaking to me and nothing more. I was confused about what happened on the ride home. And with sound judgment, I'd never trust Wind Chaser.

Where was she? I dug around Spupaleena's lodge for more food. Nothing looked good. I finished the salmon and found one bannock cake and ate that. The Native food was different than Ma's. I missed her beef stew and biscuits. Her mashed potatoes with mounds of gravy. My heart ached for home like never before. I rubbed the canoe in my pocket. It didn't help. Images of Ma scurrying around the kitchen and humming came to mind. I missed her gentle touch and Pa's nighttime prayers. My belly flip-flopped with each thought of my family. Confusion gushed over me like a torrential rainstorm. *Lord, help!*

I wandered back outside and plopped down beside

my brother. He may be younger, but somedays—and I would never admit this to him—he saw things a little more clearly than I did. "I miss Mama and Pa. And Lilly."

Delbert put aside his whittling. "I thought you liked it here. You were practically ready to marry Running Elk last time I saw ya. What happened?"

I played with a blade of grass. Broke it into little pieces. "I'm not ready to be hitched."

Delbert laughed. "I could have told ya that," he hesitated, "I saw 'im."

"Who?"

"Running Elk."

"What? When? Why didn't you tell me?"

Delbert gave me a hideous laugh. "You've been actin' like a cricket on fire since you rode up."

I could not dispute that. "What'd he say?"

Delbert fiddled with the horse he was carving. One leg emerged from the chest and he started on a second. "He said he'd come back for ya."

I snorted. "Me or Blossom?"

"Who's Blossom?"

"Never mind." I grabbed a handful of grass and tossed it. It blew back in my face.

Delbert laughed. "Still fightin' for independence?"

"Yep." I frowned at my brother. "Not certain I wanna race any longer. I'm tired of gettin' attacked. Not convinced it's worth it." I brushed off the grass.

Delbert dusted wood chips off his trousers. "Why do ya think Spupaleena kept racin'?"

Not wanting to divulge her secrets, I shrugged.

"What are ya thinkin'?"

"Not entirely certain." I turned my attention to the

horses rounding a corner in the distance, coming from the north. Pekam and Spupaleena herded them from behind. Goosebumps broke out on my arms. "Reckon I'll try a few more times."

"Figured so. It's as much a part of you as it is her." He motioned to Spupaleena with his knife.

At one time I thought that was true. It was a different life for her. Different people. Different traditions. Different times.

Chapter 25

Later that night, Spupaleena and I went for a walk. She confirmed my vision quest was nothing but wild thoughts. Anyone could have one, but mine was wishful thinking. I was fine with that. She also informed me Running Elk would not be coming back. I was right, he and Blossom were to be married in the month of hunting when leaves changed colors and warm evenings became crisp nights. Not by his will, but his father's. My heart felt as though it would tear in half.

I hated rejection—a shattered heart, tears coming and going as they pleased, emptiness. I chose to trust the Lord, knowing when I was ready He'd line me up with a suitable man. By then I'd be ready for all that goes with marriage. Or perhaps I'd stay single the rest of my life. No matter what, I'd learned life comes with compromise and sacrifice.

Spupaleena and I rested beside a creek with a slow-moving current. I shed my stockings and boots and dipped my feet in the cool water. Spupaleena did the same. The current felt as though it could wash away my sadness and confusion. I pretended to watch it drown and float down the creek, then shared my thoughts with Spupaleena. "I believe I am finished racing."

"When did you decide this?"

"I've been thinking about it for a while. Talking with you, Spotted Fawn, and Glowing Moon, I understand why each of you race. I reckon for me, it's been driven by rebellion. Even as a child."

Spupaleena swirled her toes in the water. "Why do you continue to race?"

I collected my thoughts before answering. "I reckon because I have always wanted to be like you."

Spupaleena nodded. "I love you deeply, niece. You are family to me, Pekam, Father. But you are right, rebellion feeds your desires. What does *Koolenchooten* say?"

I tossed a twig in the water. "To go home and help Pa." I laughed as a flood of relief showered over me. "I love watching my one-legged Pa work cattle as if he'd never been jumped by those thugs. Strongest man I know." I glanced at her. "But I love racing, too."

Ma and Pa told the story a little differently each time. The facts were the same: Pa and a neighbor trekked to Lincoln for supplies in the winter with four feet of snow on the ground; Mama was pregnant with me; Spupaleena was there, bruised and broken from an accident; thugs jumped the men, killing his neighbor, and Pa had to have his leg amputated.

The part that differed was how horrible the storm was and how frightened Pa had been. Pa hated to admit he was terrified for Mama and Spupaleena and me. He said the Good Lord protected us all along. It was true He had watched over us, but I knew Pa'd been fearful by the way his focus dragged to the floor when he described how he'd held Mama tightly before he walked out the door, a hitch in his voice.

"I miss my folks." This time it was me with a hitch in

my voice. "I miss Lillian, and I guess I'm not quite ready to be on my own."

"Then it is time for you to return to your family and do what *Koolenchooten* wants you to do," she turned to me, "that is a sign of becoming a woman." Spupaleena hugged me.

I held on tight to her warmth and reassurance for a moment longer than normal.

A wide grin bloomed on her face. "If you are going to stop racing, how about one more and you ride Dusty."

I sucked in a sharp breath, opened my mouth to speak, and closed it, folding my hands in my lap. "But..."

"If you are finally considering how your folks feel about all this, you need to know that while you were gone, and after time in prayer with my father, your father has agreed to leave your decision to race in *Koolenchooten's* hands. Before he and Jack came, your mother had already released you and your rebellious ways to Him."

"I needed to hear that." Peace handed me over to excitement and I smiled. "Me? Ride Dusty? But he's your champion!"

"Is there a better way to end racing than to ride, as you say, a champion?" She stood and held out her hand to me.

I grabbed hold, and she pulled me to my feet. *Me. Ride Dusty!* "Yippee!" I twirled around, hands waving in the air. Then stopped and stared at Spupaleena. "Will I be able to handle him?" *Do you want this really to be your final race?*

"We will find out."

We strolled back to Spupaleena's lodge. By the time we arrived, it was dark and the moon shone full. I found

Dusty in the meadow and combed my fingers through his tangled mane. He was mostly black and blended with the shadows, except for the white lightning bolt at the left shoulder that ran down his leg. And the patch of white that spilled over his rump and down his hip like a stretched bear claw.

I stood in the open meadow with him, yearning to connect. While he grazed, I rubbed his neck and back. Other horses came and went, sniffing and nosing me, leaving when I didn't give them much attention. I talked to Dusty and the Lord, thanking Him for one last ride when I hadn't deserved it. At the same time, my heart felt like someone was tugging on opposite ends. Race? Quit? Race? I shook my head. It was time to hang up my hat.

The next morning wasn't as promising as the night before. As I approached Dusty, he turned and trotted away. Spupaleena hollered out pointers from her mare's corral. Nothing seemed to work and I was tired of the game. Finally she whistled and he ran. Straight to her. Not the tenderfoot who chased him around the meadow.

After I'd brushed and saddled him, and was about to swing on, Spupaleena stopped me.

"Take him to the creek for a drink. Spend time with him before you ride. When you get back, you can get on," she said.

"You going to race that old grouch?" Pekam snickered and kept walking.

"What?" My voice squeaked like a little girl blowing on a broken Indian flute.

"Never mind him." Spupaleena held out the reins. "Now go."

Moonie pranced and kicked and bucked in the corral. "Settle down, girl. I'll be back." I felt bad for not racing her, but heck, who in their right mind would give up a chance to ride a legend?

I led Dusty to the creek. For an aged horse he acted spry. At the river, he plunged in, nearly ripping the reins out of my hands. When he came up for air, water dripped from his muzzle and he sighed. I stroked his white blaze. It was wide, almost the width of his nose, and long, covering from his forehead to the soft part of his muzzle. Dusty had a long, slight but rugged bump in the middle of his nose, giving him a distinct sense of charm.

I spent a short time at the creek, being anxious to ride and all, before heading back to Spupaleena. We walked a few miles to let the horses warm up before picking up speed. Dusty's body relaxed, I felt his strength beneath me. He was much older now and a little slower but I knew when the time came for him to let him loose, he would live up to his reputation. We kept on a southern trail that led us from prairie grass to sage brush.

"Time to stretch their legs." Spupaleena leaned forward and waved her feet, urging her bay colt into a faster pace.

Her colt bolted in a burst of energy. Dusty picked up speed at a more gradual pace. I did not care. I was on the back of a legend, wind in my face. After a short spell, I urged him to break from a lope into a gallop. His ears flicked back toward me, telling me he was listening and willing.

I was content with the seasoned stallion. And with Dusty's laid-back demeanor, he still out ran Moonie. The thrill of racing rushed back into my spirit, making me question my decision to quit.

Chapter 26

"Still want to quit?" Spupaleena grinned.

"I feel quitting is what the Lord wants me to do, but this feels right, too." We had been training for several weeks. I had not thought much of Running Elk or Wind Chaser. The urgency to be on my own dissipated with each day. But the struggle to give up racing tore at me.

"Race and see what happens. I will support you no matter what you choose."

Her words released a straggling pressure I did not realize I had. The upcoming race was in eight days. We finished the routine and headed back to Spupaleena's lodge. I had much to ponder. I prayed most of the way back, asking for guidance. I did not like asking for His will, as the Lord's Prayer suggested. It tended to get in my way. That's what Mama called stubborn pride. It's what I called comfortable.

"I think we need to add shooting bows and knife throwing. Make things tougher," Spupaleena said. "Men do not like changes. We can use this against them."

"You've seen me shoot off a horse." I shake my head. "No, ma'am!"

"*Kewa*. You can do this. I *have* seen you shoot. You are as good as anyone."

"With a rifle, perhaps. Not bow and arrow. And knives? We've not practiced!" I pressed a hand to my throat. "Oh, Falling Rain wants to come with us and race too."

"I do not think she will be going anywhere. Her father is back," Spupaleena said.

I glanced down, thinking about the reasons why he would have come back early. With a sigh, I nodded. It was safer for her to remain with her pa. It was not my place to come between the two of them.

"*Kewa.* We will ride in the mornings and you will practice with your bow and knife in the evenings with Pekam."

"He won't agree."

"Trust me. He will."

Spupaleena kicked her horse into a trot.

We trained hard the following six days. Each day I rode Dusty and several other of Spupaleena's and Pekam's horses, seasoned and colts.

"If you can ride many horses well, you can ride one horse effortlessly," Pekam said.

The end of day seven staggered in. I felt both exhausted and confident. I'd hit my marks fairly consistently, and Dusty galloped with speed and spunk like when he was younger.

Pekam found us a cool, grassy spot away from the village to practice shooting bows and tossing knives. Crickets chirped as if to praise our accomplishments. The air was hot and dry, almost stifling, and the sky was dark blue, not yet painted dusk's orange and purple. I steadied myself and pulled back the bow. When I was about to let the arrow loose, the string busted and the bow jerked back, leaving a huge welt on my right eye. My vision blurred in that eye, and tears streamed down my cheeks from pain and frustration.

"Go soak it with river water." Pekam found me a scrap of buckskin. "Use this."

I took it from him, handed him my bow and arrow, and headed for the river.

"I'll find Smilkameen."

I waved without glancing back at him. How would I ever be able race now? Shooting and knife tossing was out of the question. We were scheduled to leave at first light. I was convinced this was the Lord's confirmation—to give up racing was the right answer.

Wind Chaser was nowhere in sight. I ran toward his brother, calling for Wind Chaser. With a startled look on his face, the boy spun around, lost his balance, and tumbled into the water. I dropped the buckskin cloth and sprinted toward him. I yelled again for Wind Chaser. Ran. Yelled. Prayed. Ran. My legs would not carry me fast enough.

When I reached the water, I dove in. I could not find the boy. I feared the current had already carried him away. Blurred by water and swelling, I dove in again. And again, swimming in circles, reaching, searching. Finally, I felt an arm, grabbed hold, and pulled his body to the surface. Wind Chaser grabbed his brother from me, accusing me of trying to drown the little one. With a twisted expression he screamed at me, shoving me backward.

"I helped him." I reached out for the boy.

Wind Chaser shoved me again, this time I fell into the water. The boy cried and clung to his brother.

Wind Chaser continued to yell at me, a fist in the air.

"No!" I shook my head. "I saw him down here alone." I pointed to my eye. "I was coming for cold water. He was alone. I called for you. Did you not hear me?" Fresh tears trickled down my face. "He fell!" I pointed to the river. "He fell! I saved him."

Pekam rushed into the water, standing between me and Wind Chaser. They debated, pointed at me, the water, back at me. I stood, shaking my head.

"He fell. I was helping him." Why would this monster not listen to me? I would not ever harm a soul. Especially a child.

Wind Chaser held his brother tight and stormed back toward the village. He spoke soothingly to his brother, rubbing his back.

I turned to Pekam. "He fell."

"I believe you." Pekam put a hand on my shoulder. "Are you all right?"

I shivered, sobbing. "No…"

Pekam drew me into his arms. "His brother is safe. He is scared. In time, he will see you tried to help."

"No. He won't! Why does he hate me so much?"

"He does not hate you. He hates himself." Pekam led me to the shore.

"Why?"

"It is not for me to say."

I retrieved my buckskin and soaked it in the water, pressing it to my eye. Not only did my eye ache, but now so did my head.

Chapter 27

I waited on the hot sand while Pekam fetched medicine, digging with my feet in search of a cool spot. Soft footsteps sounded behind me. I didn't want to see anyone, especially the grumpy healer. I drew my knees up and hugged them, hiding my face.

"How is your eye?" She sat down beside me.

I jerked my face up enough to peer through the cracks of a bent elbow.

Falling Rain's expression revealed compassion. She gave me a small grin. Normally her long hair was tightly braided. Today it hung loose, cascading over her shoulders and down her back. With round, tanned face and glowing skin, it is what I imagined an angel would look like.

"Where is your father?" I said.

"Hunting."

"What are you doing here? I thought you were forbidden to talk to me."

"I was."

"Oh?" A pinch of hope swirled around me.

"I don't know what changed his mind. *Koolenchooten* may have carved some of his stubbornness away." She grinned.

"He had plenty of it."

"He likes people to think he is mean and tough. He is not as strong as he pretends to be. Even though he is easily angered, by sundown he is nothing more than a huggable cottontail."

I swirled circles in the sand with a finger. "I miss my folks."

"Are you going home?"

I nodded. "Soon."

"After the race?" Sorrow filled her voice.

"How did you know?"

"I spoke with Spupaleena a few suns ago, and just now saw Pekam. He told me you were down here." She hesitated, playing with the fringe on her doeskin dress. "I want to race, too."

"No!" I swung the palm of my hand toward her face. "You will be punished."

"My father will be away until after the race. I want to race one time. That is all. *Naux*." She held up one finger.

"No. It's too big a risk."

"A risk? It is a risk for you." Falling Rain lifted her chin. "I am strong. I will not get hurt."

I fingered my canoe. "I do not want your Pa to send you away like Calling Bird did to Running Elk. I could not bear that."

"I will worry about him." She broke out into a smirk. "I have been training." She slipped a small bone knife out of her moccasin and handed it to me.

I took it, knowing she was stubborn enough to follow though. "I'm training so hard it hurts." I turned my face to her and pointed to my eye.

Falling Rain gasped.

"I cannot race now." I pressed the damp buckskin to my eye. "You can take my place."

"Does it hurt?"

"Everything is fuzzy."

Falling Rain stood. "We need to find Smilkameen."

I groaned, swirled my scrap of buckskin in the river, and followed her to the village, a sliver of light leading the way. We could not find the grumpy healer anywhere. So we searched for Pekam, hoping he'd caught up to her, and found him chewing on a fist-sized hunk of dried salmon outside his lodge.

He took a long drink of water and nodded at us. "I see you found each other." He tossed me a pouch. "Have some."

I took out two pieces of salmon and handed one to Falling Rain. "Did you find the healer?"

In between bites Pekam said, "I could not find her. She must be somewhere gathering medicine. I believe Spupaleena is off praying somewhere."

My eye stung, making me as grumpy as Smilkameen. I pressed the buckskin scrap against my eye with one hand and held my pounding head with the other. "I'm not gonna race. I can't…"

"You will be fine. Go lay down. When you wake up you will feel better."

I chewed the last bite of salmon. "I reckon you're right."

Pekam smiled. "I am always right."

I had my doubts. The swelling in my eye would eventually diminish,

CHAPTER 28

Headache gone, I scurried off my tule-mat bed the morning of the race and hurried out of the lodge. My vision was still slightly blurred, so I slowed down after a few steps.

Smilkameen trudged up to me and handed me a scrap of buckskin with a spot of liquid in the middle "Put this on your eye." She spoke in Sinyekst.

I pressed it against my eyelid and thanked her. She shuffled away, back hunched. Stomach churning, I skipped my morning meal and went in search of Dusty. He was not in his corral. Panic surged through me. I rubbed my wooden canoe and scanned the area for my runaway horse. He was not with Spupaleena's horses. Nor with Pekam's. *Where could he have disappeared to?*

I jogged south, to the shady spot I often see horses in the afternoon. He wasn't there. I turned and sprinted to the river. No sign of him. *Where are Spupaleena and Pekam?* Breathless, I strode back to her lodge. In the distance, Pekam led Dusty with a twisted hemp rope around his neck, Spupaleena beside him.

Bent over to catch my breath, I thanked the Lord. I made my way to the corral. Uncle handed me the rope. "Where did you find him?" I pressed a hand to my side.

"By the creek." Pekam pointed north.

I examined the corral rails. "How did he get out?"

"He must have jumped," Spupaleena said. "He found five girlfriends to visit. I did not recognize the mares."

I examined the horizon to the north, as if I could see the mares. "I'm surprised they didn't follow you." I put him back in the corral.

"They tried. I chased them off." Spupaleena slid off her horse.

Pekam slapped the top pole with his rope. Dusty jumped and ran in circles.

My body trembled as he spiraled around and kicked up his back hooves. "Is he gonna stay like that for the race?"

Spupaleena shook her head. "He will settle down."

What happened to my meek stallion? His muscles trembled as he called out to the mares. Head and tail high in the air, he paced in the small space. He called again, this time rearing up like he was going to jump the rails. Pekam put his hands high in the air and shouted to him.

"When are we leaving?" I swallowed the fear gathering in my throat.

"Soon. We will travel north most of the day." Spupaleena motioned upriver with her head. "That will settle him down." She opened the gate. "Get him ready."

"Will he be too tired to race?" I walked through the gate, not wanting to be in the cramped space with a rearing, wild-eyed stallion.

Spupaleena shook her head. "*Loot*. We will race in the morning after the horses are rested."

"But I thought we were racing today." I gripped his halter with white knuckles.

"We will race in the morning," Pekam repeated. "Some of the men will not arrive until tonight."

"I reckon I can wait." With raised hands, I spoke in a soft tone. "Easy, boy."

Spupaleena laughed. She closed the gate. "I have not seen you make that face since you were this high." She tapped her knee.

I suddenly felt that high. "Can we practice shooting bows tonight?" I kept my gaze on Dusty. How could I give this up?

"*Kewa*," Pekam said. "And knife throwing. You need it." The sound of his voice implied he was teasing.

Dusty settled down enough for me to slip the halter over his head. I brushed and saddled him.

"Go eat," Spupaleena said. "You will need your strength."

My mind drifted to Mama's fried eggs, bacon, and flapjacks. Spupaleena was out of the flour she'd traded for with Mama, or I'd make some. Day old bannock with huckleberry sauce would have to suit me.

I figured we'd have trouble riding past the mares that had been near the creek, but they were nowhere in sight. Dusty's ears swiveled back and forth as we rode by, searching for his band of girls, I reckoned. He pranced a few steps, so I circled him around a few times until he settled back into his smooth cadence.

We followed the Columbia River most of the day and by the time we reached a T on the trail, my backside was stiff and sore. It felt like I was sittin' on blisters.

I'd never been this far north on this side of the Columbia. Mountains rose high on either side of the river. Still miles away, the falls where they fished for salmon rumbled. Fir and pine trees coated the hills with tamarack interspersed here and there. Yellow sunflowers and other purple, white, and orange wildflowers cascaded the hills. Knee-high, tan grass swept the earth.

"This is the perfect spot!" I slid off Dusty, picked a purple flower, and smelled it.

Spupaleena smiled. "We will race over there." She pointed west, where a wide trail curved around a bend in the distance, trees lining the way.

"I hoped we would camp here for the night." I sighed.

Spupaleena shook her head. "We will stay here for a while and pray. Then ride toward the mountains and camp by the creek."

Five men on horses approached. With them was Silent Thunder, Standing Bear, and Wind Chaser. They walked their horses past, glaring at me and Spupaleena.

"Don't say a word. Just let them pass," Pekam whispered.

They snaked their way up the trail. I tied Dusty to a tree. Nose bumping his side, he seemed agitated. I swatted bugs away and massaged his back, jittery myself.

We formed a circle on the ground, legs crossed, and prayed. Prayed for safety, wisdom, and strength. I prayed for protection against those who wanted to hurt me. My mind had a hard time focusing. All I could think about was Wind Chaser accusing me of trying to drown his brother. Time seemed to drag on. When finished, I went to fetch my horse. He stomped his back foot, biting at his side. He had a look of pain in his eyes. I checked his feet and legs. All seemed fine.

We rode west toward the mountains along a swift-moving creek. The sound of water crashing over boulders racked my nerves. Every threat those boys had made against me battered my brain. I tipped my Stetson back on my head, allowing fresh air to caress my skin.

It didn't take us long to reach camp. We unloaded saddles and supplies in a grassy spot near the creek. A good-sized crowd gathered at the base of the northern mountain range. About fifteen of those were riders. Half of them came from the Pend Oreille River territory—the *Kalispeliwho* or Brown Camas People. French trappers referred to them as the river paddlers. The others were *Spukanee*—The Children of the Sun—and lived roughly eighty-five miles southeast of my cabin.

After talking with a handful of the racers, Spupaleena came over. "Thirty more racers are on their way."

I caught a glimpse of Wind Chaser. The same angry look smeared across his face, as if ready to attack the first person to bump into him. My gut churned like Mama's butter-making machine. Over and over. I won't miss him.

Pekam stepped behind me and whispered, "Use your knife if you have to."

I swallowed, uncertain if he was serious or not.

Spupaleena placed a hand on my shoulder. "You are ready. Remember, ride with Dusty. Trust *Koolenchooten*." She went over to a group of elders and greeted them in the usual traditional way—introducing herself and her family line.

Some of the men wore their hair loose and others with only the hair closest to their face in thin braids. I could not tell one tribe from the other. I examined Pekam and the boys, trying to find variances. Only in speech could I tell a difference. They used a great deal of hand signals with spoken words to communicate.

Then I glanced at their horses. Some had what looked like layers of water ripples and others had sun painted on their rumps. Spupaleena, I knew, wore three purple crosses on her horse's rump and three eagle feathers tied in a line down the mane when she relay raced. Pekam's horses wore a blue hand print on their hind ends.

I turned to Pekam. "Are we gonna paint Dusty?"

Pekam arched his brows. "What do you mean paint him?"

"Like them?" I pointed to the other horses. I caught Wind Chaser glaring at me, but pretended not to let it bother me as I fingered my canoe.

"*Loot.* They came here from a relay race."

Part of me was disappointed. I would have chosen red, the color of the living blood that ran through our veins. A canoe resembled my journey with the Sinyekst. With Running Elk and Falling Rain. With Moonie and Dusty. With Spupaleena. And *Koolenchooten.*

"If you were to paint him, what would it look like?" Pekam asked.

I told him.

"Mmm. Strong medicine."

Pekam and I spent the rest of the evening shooting bows and throwing knives on the south side of the creek. My mind jumped to Wind Chaser between shots and throws. When done I sat on a rock and imagined I was paddling my canoe, gliding across smooth water, Dusty's reflection staring back at me.

I glanced at him. He was more agitated than before, pawing the ground. I untied his lead and walked him around. He must be as nervous as me. Once he seemed calmer, I tied him firmly to a tree and settled in for the night.

Chapter 29

With heavy lids, I blinked awake. Trees cast shadows from the half-moon's illumination.

Spupaleena stirred as if dreaming about her past.

Pekam rolled over. "You awake?"

"Can't sleep." I'd never felt this restless.

"Why not?"

"Reckon I'm as nervous as a rabbit runnin' from a coyote." I sat up. "Best go check on Dusty."

"These boys you are racing are not coyotes. They are fluffy bunnies. You are the fierce wolf, leader of the pack. And with Dusty, those bunnies will be wetting the ground, trying to keep up with you. Eating his dust. You know that is why Jack named him what he did?"

"I've heard that story for years." I was the horrified bunny. "I'll be back."

I picked my way through the brush and rocks to check on Dusty. He lay motionless, not even lifting his head as I approached. "Dusty…" I whispered. No movement. I pressed a hand to my chest. My heartbeat raced. "Dusty." This time I spoke a little louder. Shivers crawled up my arms. I tiptoed toward him in case I was wrong and he was sleeping.

I lay a trembling hand on his neck. He was cold. Stiff.

"Dusty!" I screamed, unable to move at first. Then I shook him, begging him to stand. Hasty footsteps sounded behind me.

"What is it?" Pekam knelt beside Dusty.

"Get up!" I sobbed, trying to figure out what was wrong. Was he sick? Was that why he was agitated yesterday? I should have told Spupaleena. "I thought he was nervous."

Pekam laid a hand on my shoulder. "He's dead." He sat back on his heels. "How did he act last night?"

"Last night?" Spupaleena dropped to her knees by his head. "Was he sick?" She stroked his nose.

"He kept nosing his belly. I swatted bugs away…" I lay on his shoulder, a deep moan slipping from my throat. "What have I done?'

"If he was sick, there was nothing anyone could have done," Pekam said.

Spupaleena helped me up and led me back to camp. "Lay down. Pekam and I need to take care of Dusty. We will figure something out."

I curled into a ball and closed my stinging eyes. My mind fixated on Dusty's motionless form. His icy, rigid body under my fingers. There was no way I'd race today. Or ever again. This had to be the Lord's punishment for my rebellious ways.

By the time Spupaleena and Pekam returned, everyone was awake and almost ready to begin. Several men had joined them, making the task of burial light.

Pekam motioned to a tule mat full of roasted camas. "Eat."

"I'm not hungry."

He shoved some in my hands. "You will ride

Spupaleena's colt. You need your strength."

I shook my head. "I can't—"

"You will! This is part of racing. It is part of raising horses. We are born to die." He motioned for me to eat. "You want to be a woman? Here is your chance."

I bit off a small piece, tears tumbling down my face.

"Dry your tears. They will not help Dusty."

I mopped my face with my shirtsleeve.

"This is your journey. Take it." Spupaleena spoke from behind me.

I mustered the strength to finish the camas cake. She was right. This was my journey. No one could steal it from me, and I was not about to hand it over to those no-account boys.

"I used to feel like there was no way could I beat my sister—the warrior woman racer—known all over the land," Pekam said. "Then one day I did win. You can win."

With trembling fingers, I smoothed back loose strands of hair from my face. "I am scared. All I can think about is Dusty. It's my fault." I yanked on my boot laces.

"No one is to blame." He smiled at me. "I will race first, giving you time to ride the colt. Spupaleena will help."

I nodded. "You saw how bad my knife throwing was last night. How can I win?"

"Today is new." He placed both hands on my shoulders. "See the knife hit the mark and it will." He pulled an arrow out of my quiver. "Your arrows and knife have yellow stripes, so we will know where they land."

Spupaleena strode over. "It is time. Come, we need

to circle around my colt and ask for *Koolenchooten's* blessings."

The colt took in a deep breath, snorting it out. He held his head high, pawing the ground. On his rump was a red canoe floating on blue water. I turned to Pekam. "Did you paint him?"

He grinned. "Every racer needs a symbol."

The symbol stood out boldly on both sides. I stoked the colt's nose. "I trust you."

We formed a circle around him, laid our hands on his body, and prayed, asking for protection.

"Get your saddle, *Kook Yuma Mahooya*." Spupaleena pointed to the boys who were lining up. "Or you will miss the race."

I grabbed a brush and ran it over his back. Pekam slapped the colt's muscles to warm them up since we were out of time. I threw the saddle on and cinched it tight. The metal bar of his bridle clinked his teeth, and I winced. The colt opened his mouth wider and I slid the bit in. "Sorry, boy. I'm tryin' to slow down." Once the bridle was on, I hopped into the saddle and walked up to the others.

Seven boys riding bareback with a string around their horses' jaws stared at me as if I'd come for war. I felt like slithering off my saddle and slinking back to the village. Instead, knowing this was a piece of my rite of passage, I lifted my chin and narrowed my eyes. I turned my attention to an elder with a hand drum standing to the side of us. Like the other men and boys, he wore leggings and moccasins. An eagle feather topped a single braid that ran down the length of his back. He stood shorter than most men. But he had a confidence in him that matched his deep voice.

I patted my pocket, making certain my knife was in its place. Then realized I'd forgotten my bow and arrows. I felt heat rise up my neck.

"Hannah," a hushed voice said.

I turned to see Pekam holding out my bow and quiver filled with five arrows. Snickers filled the air as I grabbed them from my uncle. I slid the quiver and bow over my shoulders, adjusting for ease of extraction. The colt fidgeted, bumping into those on either side of us. I backed him up, reined him around, and slipped back in my spot. He pawed, shaking his head.

Wind Chaser rode up and halted on one side of me, Silent Thunder on the other. Three boys were between me and Standing Bear. All glared at me. I kept my gaze in front of me. *Focus on the ride.* My tummy roiled, and I thought I might lose the camas cakes.

Thankfully, I knew enough of the hand gestures to understand the course. My thoughts bounced from images of my knife throwing the previous night—which led me to believe I couldn't hit the side of Pa's barn—to Dusty's dead body. I fought back tears. I forced myself to think about the first leg of this race—jumping over a series of downed trees.

Two whacks of the drum jolted me. The colt reared. Wind Chaser and Silent Thunder squeezed us in. The next whack would be the signal to go. I bit my lip, running the course through my mind as Spupaleena had shared that morning, and waited.

Chapter 30

Horses pranced, slamming into each other. Held toward the middle, I had little room to maneuver. I elbowed Winder Chaser and Silent Thunder as they crowded me. It felt as though I rode on a slim raft during a squall. Just as I shoved Silent Thunder away from me, the drummer whacked his drum with a single beat, and we bolted into the clearing, headed for the tree line that would take us up the mountain. The colt lurched, knocking me to the side. I grabbed the horn and pulled myself back into the center of the saddle.

Wind Chaser took the lead. I was four riders behind. I pinned my gaze on the back of one boy in front of me whose horse had a yellow sun stamped on his rump. We came to a wide, low spot in the creek and ran our horses through. Water splashed on my legs and face, blurring my vision.

Sun Boy veered right, and I was able to inch closer to him. After jumping several downed logs, we headed toward the base of a tall hill, and wound our way to the top. Our horses slowed as we crowned the peak, digging into the dirt with their hooves. Powerful muscles bunched. Sweat slid off their flanks. The colt was more sure-footed than I'd remembered. He dug, lunged, dug, lunged.

On top we picked through several horse lengths of rock. Once across, the horses sped up, arched to the left, and wound down the south side. Near the bottom, we navigated a fragment that was as steep as a cow's face. I leaned back—almost on the colt's rump—and inched him past Sun Boy and one other rider. I caught up to Standing Bear.

Upon breaking into a clearing, the colt shifted into a speed I'd not yet ridden, and we passed Standing Bear. I followed Wind Chaser and Silent Thunder back over the fallen logs. Standing Bear's horse huffed behind me. At this point I no longer feared them. We could win. All I had to do now was hit my marks. I'd done it in the past. There was no reason I could not hit them today.

The colt jumped over three remaining weathered logs scattered across the earth. We headed the short distance to the creek and surged through, passing Silent Thunder. A high-pitched shrill escaped through my bared teeth, urging the colt forward. We climbed up the bank and ran for the target area.

I reined the colt to a slower speed and tugged my knife out of the pocket of my riding skirt. I could tell he was exhausted. "Almost there," I said. With steady fingers, I placed the sheath between my teeth, slid the knife out, and found my target. I had one shot. I said a quick prayer and flung it. From the sharp *thwack* I knew it stuck. There was not enough time to fiddle with the sheath so I kept it in my mouth.

Breaths hard and fast, the colt remained at the slower pace on his own, which pleased me as I needed the balance to slide my bow from my back. Which I did with no complications and fitted an arrow to the string. Wind

Chaser was a hair ahead of me. On the opposite side, he shot his first arrow. I heard the *thwack*. It sent apprehension into the battle-field of my mind.

To fight off the tension, I imagined myself in a canoe, gliding across calm waters. A bald eagle soared above, dropping courage into my soul. His wing span settled over me—protection sent from *Koolenchooten,* I was certain. With his series of high-pitched *Kuk, Kuk, Kuk* sounds, I felt he was telling me my time was near. In my mind I paddled hard to keep up with him. He circled above. I readied my bow below.

With narrow eyes, I pinned my sights on the first target: a leaf stuck to a tree with sap. With one fluid motion, I aimed, pulled back, and let the arrow loose. I shot four more arrows, one after the other, and galloped toward the finish point, which was between the two men we rode past at the start of the race.

When we passed the line, our horses were nose to nose. It was too close to tell. The colt's sides heaved. Thick white lather soaked Wind Chaser's horse's chest and under his tail. I reined him down to a walk, weaving in and out of trees, allowing him to cool off and catch his breath. I took that time to thank the Lord for allowing me to ride such a thrilling, final race. And with a powerful, big-hearted horse. A peace covered me like no other. I had no idea how long I'd have to wait to find out who won. Or how the elder would tell us.

When the colt's breathing shallowed and some of the sweat dried, I handed him off to Pekam and found Spupaleena. She was in the middle of a group of arguing men. My name was shouted above the whir of voices. So was Wind Chaser's. I glanced at him. He bored a look of disgust into me. Our two names were lobbed back and forth until a sudden silence struck the air.

Spupaleena waved me over. One of the men motioned to Wind Chaser. I strolled over with my head high, trying to hide my wobbly legs. I rubbed the canoe for strength and calm.

The drummer lined the eight of us up in the middle of the crowd. The onlookers raised their hands and war-whooped. It made me blush like the morning dawn. Spupaleena stood beside me, shoulders back. A large man with one abalone earring and loose hair—I assumed a leader of some sort—spoke in his dialect, pointing a turtle rattle with long fringe strung with trading beads at both me and Wind Chaser. Spupaleena interpreted.

"*Koolenchooten* has blessed these two young people with strength and heart of warriors." He talked about the honor of horse racing and how it blessed the people spiritually. He talked about woman breaking out of tradition. He did not comment if he favored it or not. He told a story of a young warrior no taller than a grasshopper who went into battle and fought off giants with his bow and a handful of arrows. He deemed it was the boy's training that conquered the giants.

I listened, thinking about David killing Goliath in the Bible. It was also his training that slayed the giant. The Lord had prepared him years ahead of time. I could not help but ponder what He was preparing me for. Even though racing felt right, I had a peace that surpasses all understanding. A peace only the Lord could supply me with. I knew I'd miss it, but understood my decision was the right one.

The leader explained the history of horse racing and how important horses were to the People. He concluded with, "These two are both skillful riders, but only one can win."

I glanced at Spupaleena, thankful she'd ridden before me and all the other girls, clearing new paths for us to take.

"I have this turtle rattle," he lifted it in the air, "and I will hand it to the winner." He studied us both with a somber face. After closing his eyes for a few moments, he opened them and stepped forward.

With doubt squeezing my chest I glanced down, certain Wind Chaser had won. I would return home, empty handed, ready to live out expected obligations. I tried to exhale a calming breath. It was time to surrender childish ways. The leader's moccasins came into view. He handed the rattle to me. I gasped and looked up. He smiled, speaking in his dialect, both of our fingers wrapped around the handle. I did not know what he'd said, but I understood the meaning without Spupaleena having to interpret. He regarded me with pride and honor, something I was not used to from a male racer. Red faced, Wind Chaser turned to me, gave a curt nod, and stomped off. The other boys did the same.

I swallowed. "Much obliged, sir." I extended my hand.

He glanced at Spupaleena with a quizzical expression on his face.

She motioned for him to shake my hand.

The crowd dispersed. Wind Chaser and the others huddled in a tight circle. A pit formed in my stomach. I held the rattle to my chest. "Lord, don't let them come after me."

Chapter 31

"Time to gather our belongings and head back," Pekam said. "You won. I won." He held up some of the loot he acquired from his win: tanned hides, jerked buffalo meat, beads.

I fingered a red and blue beaded necklace.

"Take it." Pekam slipped the necklace over my head. "And all of that." He pointed behind me.

I gasped. "That's all mine?"

"And so is she." Spupaleena joined us, handing me a rope attached to a stout, appaloosa mare one of the male racers had wagered on Wind Chaser. Eyes big and gentle, she reached out her nose and sniffed me. I rubbed her dark face and neck. Most of her body was the color of nighttime shadows with only patches of white and black spots over her rump. I'd never imagined owning such a magnificent animal.

I kept one eye on the boys huddled together in a tight circle as I packed my belongings. The urge to get away from any potential revenge pushed me to work quickly. We rolled our loot in blankets, buckskin, and hemp rope and tied it all onto the back of our saddles. I admired the mare before mounting. "You're beautiful."

In order to get the boys out of my mind, I thought

of names for my mare as we rode down the trail. *Spirit. Freckles. Lacey. Spot.*

"Have you decided what you are going to do?" Spupaleena said.

Eyes on the mare's slick, black mane, I sighed. "I reckon the boys ain't gonna stop harassin' me. It's time to go home and stay put for a while." I glanced at my Sinyekst relatives. "Thank you for leading me on this journey."

Pekam chuckled. "It will be a good story to tell your children."

"I may not want to share it with them." I wrinkled my nose. "Not certain I want horse-lovin' daughters."

Pekam and Spupaleena laughed.

Spupaleena turned serious. "You have come a long way with your decision. I think you are now listening to *Koolenchooten*."

"I'm trying. It's time to go home and help Pa with the ranch."

"You can also work on your knife throwing." Pekam leaned over and in a teasing manner, shoved my arm.

I shoved him back. "I never did get a looksee of where my knife and arrow hit the targets."

Pekam made an O shape with his mouth. "I forgot to tell you."

"No matter. I left them behind." I slapped my leg.

"I have them," Spupaleena said. "The boys collected and sorted them out. I am sorry we did not tell you."

I groaned. "That's what they were doing?"

"What did you think was going on?" Spupaleena handed me my knife.

I fingered the yellow stripe. "I thought they were

planning their revenge."

"That is why you were eager to leave." Pekam tilted his head back and laughed. "I thought maybe you fancied one of them."

"No!" I pursed my lips. "Not a one." My heart yearned for Running Elk. Even though I was not ready to wed, he was the one I desired. I could not imagine marrying anyone else.

"They were embarrassed to lose to a girl, but they were not going to harm you." Spupaleena handed me my arrows. "They were licking their wounds as a dog licks his."

I poked Pekam with an arrow. "Is that how you felt losing to your sister?"

"I was more proud of her than ashamed. It made me work harder." He smiled at Spupaleena. "I wanted to be like her."

"Never." Spupaleena returned the gesture. "You are a fine rider, *Sintahoos*. You make me proud."

"So, how did I do?"

"You hit the mark." Pekam smiled at me, pride covering his face.

I clutched the rattle to my chest. It was time to go home. I longed to hear Mama hum while she cooked and dried her herbs. Looked forward to dirt-covered hands as we worked side by side in her garden. To ride alongside Pa and Delbert. Play with Lillian and teach the importance of following the Lord's lead. I rode the rest of the way to the village with a peaceful heart, knowing a new journey was about to begin.

Acknowledgments

My appreciation to Becky England for proofing yet another manuscript.

Thanks to Heidi Thomas for your wonderful edits and suggestions. You always make my writing deeper and tighter.

Thanks to Joe, my terrific husband, who supports my writing and horse frolicking dreams. Thank you for marrying me and bringing me to your reservation, giving me a chance to share its wonder and beauty and culture with the world.

Thanks to my writer friends, Christy Martenson and Violet Gulack, for your continued support and inspiration.

Glossary of Sinyekst Words Used in Hannah's Journey

Sinyekst (modern is Sinixt): Speckled Fish/Bull Trout
Spupaleena: Rabbit
Pekam: Bobcat
Toom: Mother
Mistum: Father
Kewa: yes
Naux: one
Loot: no
Kook Yuma Mahooya: Tiny Raccoon
Koolenchooten: God
Sweenompt iss stoonhuh: Handsome is Beaver.
Wha Whelwho: Fox
cha hooy-huh: come here
Hahoolawho: Rattle Snake
Skumheist: Bear
Smilkameen: Swan
Kukneeya: listen
Uks kawup oalth host: Your horse is good.
Ninawees: see you later
Wussa: aunt
Kalispeliwho: Kalispel
Spukanee: Spokane
Host: good
naux new: one more
naux: one
aseel: two

Where to Find Carmen Peone

Website: http://carmenpeone.com/

Facebook: https://www.facebook.com/CarmenEPeone

Twitter: https://twitter.com/carmenpeone

Pinterest: https://www.pinterest.com/carmenpeone/

Amazon: https://www.amazon.com/Carmen-Peone/e/B00A92O4R4